THINGS NOT SEEN

DERINDA BABCOCK

Cover and Interior Design: Derinda Babcock

Editor(s): Helene Smith

PUBLISHED BY: 4Him Press, P.O.Box 127, Marvel, CO 81329, 2023

Library Cataloging Data

Names: Babcock, Derinda (Derinda Babcock)

Things Not Seen / Derinda Babcock

162 p. 23cm × 15cm (9in × 6 in.)

Identifiers: ISBN-13: 9780990439875 (paperback) | 9780990439882 (trade hardcover) | 9780990439899 (e-book)

Key Words: survival; plane crash; mountain man; pilot; Colorado Rocky Mountains; heiress; clean and wholesome romance

Library of Congress Control Number: 2023912857 Fiction

Now faith is the substance of things hoped for,
the evidence of things not seen.
Hebrews 11:1 (KJV)

CHAPTER 1

BELLE opened her eyes. She stared at the branches overhead and struggled to focus. *Branches?*

Memory returned as pain raced through every muscle in her body and settled in her head. The terrible storm. The lightning strike. The disabled aircraft. The plane's sudden lurch and plunge toward the earth. Screams. Cries to God for mercy. Tearing, ripping, and the odor of jet fuel and blood. The woman in the seat across from her—so pretty, but now so mangled and lifeless.

Belle closed her eyes and tried not to remember the sight of bodies and airplane parts strewn all over the mountain valley when she first gained consciousness, but they were indelibly imprinted on her brain.

She shuddered, and bile climbed into her throat. Why hadn't she taken a different flight from Denver? She'd be safe at home now in her parents' cozy penthouse in Dallas instead of sprawled under a tree somewhere high in the Colorado Rockies.

Groaning, she tried to sit up. Cold enveloped her as soon as she moved, so she curled back into a fetal position and shivered uncontrollably. The smell of jet fuel sickened her.

"Here, this should help."

She opened her eyes and stared into the face of a young blond man with gentle brown eyes and dark eyebrows. He couldn't be more than twenty. Cuts and bruises emphasized the paleness of his face.

He draped a coat over her and smiled. "I'm Liam Swanson. Captain Sutherland and Mr. Morgan are trying to get a fire started. We'll be warmer soon."

Her voice had no strength, so the words came out in a whisper. "Thanks. I'm Arabella St. John. Call me Belle." Her teeth chattered. "I'm so cold."

Liam hesitated. "Do you think you'd be warmer if I sat next to you and shared my heat?"

She eyed the young man before nodding. "Please."

He eased himself down beside her, and she struggled to sit up. He helped her and put his arm around her shoulders. His hug offered limited warmth.

"What if you slide onto my lap, Belle? I promise I'm not a pervert. I can keep most of your back warm. We'll use the extra coat to wrap around the front of us."

The cold seeped into Belle's bones. Without a word, she slid onto Liam's lap.

He unzipped his jacket and drew her against his sweater-clad chest before covering them with the extra coat and wrapping his arms around her.

Immediately, heat enveloped her. She sighed and wished she could make herself small enough to fit her legs and feet inside this warm space. She leaned her head against Liam's shoulder and closed her eyes. The shivering stopped, and sleep called to her.

"Belle, Captain Sutherland and Mr. Morgan started a fire. Do you want to go and warm yourself?" Liam whispered near Belle's ear. His voice sounded strained.

She didn't want to move, but as her senses returned, Belle realized Liam must be stiff from holding her and sitting in one position for she didn't know how long. She slid off his lap. "Thanks for sharing."

His smile twisted into a grimace. "You're welcome." He stood and shook and stomped the circulation back into his limbs.

Belle approached the fire, and two men looked up. Both were cut and bruised.

The thirtysomething man in the pilot's uniform stood. "How do you feel, Miss?"

Her eyes met his blue ones. She wrapped her arms around herself and shivered. "Like I've been in a plane crash, Captain Sutherland."

He nodded. "Come closer to the fire. Do you feel any lumps or bumps indicating you have head trauma?"

Belle examined her head with a careful touch. "No, but I do have a headache."

"Your name?"

"Belle St. John."

Sutherland indicated the man who fed sticks into the fire. "This is Mr. Morgan."

The brown-haired man looked up. His intense green eyes met hers. He scanned her face and form before nodding. "Miss St. John." He then refocused on the fire.

His aloof gaze and cool tone dismissed her. Belle stiffened. Had the man made a snap judgment about her worth as a person based solely on her looks? People had done the same thing to her many times in the past, and her resentment flared.

She'd had to fight for respect from the time she put on the first hint of eye shadow and mascara and realized her long, blond hair, brown eyes, and feminine form garnered admiring glances from males and jealous looks from females. She couldn't count the number of times she'd been called *Barbie doll* in mocking tones.

In school, she'd had to work extra hard at everything she did to prove she had brains as well as looks.

Liam placed the extra coat around her, then rubbed his hands together and held them over the flames. She stepped to his side.

They all looked up when thunder rumbled and lightning lit the ominous-looking clouds.

Morgan added more wood and stood. "We need to create a shelter before we get drenched, Captain. Only a few hours of daylight remain."

Sutherland nodded. "Can you and Liam handle this while Miss St. John and I go through the wreckage to see if we can find anything to eat or drink?"

"Yes. Watch for my rifle case too. We're going to need an edge."

"Will do." Sutherland turned toward the broken plane resting at a distance from the fire. "Come, Miss St. John. We're looking for anything that might mean the difference between us living or dying. Food, water, clothing, containers of any kind, medicine."

She nodded and followed him in silence. Moving warmed her. As they neared the plane, the smell of jet fuel grew stronger.

"Should we be this close? Is there any chance the plane will catch on fire from all the leaked fuel?"

He didn't look at her when he answered. "Jet fuel is highly flammable and can ignite with a spark, but the fuel's flashpoint is high."

"Which means?"

"The flashpoint is the temperature at which the fuel begins to vaporize and ignite when exposed to a spark or flame. If we had hundred-degree Fahrenheit weather or a heat source that would reach this temperature or higher, we'd significantly increase the chance of an explosion."

Belle shivered. "So, you're saying the fuel isn't easily ignited in this cold weather?"

"Yes, but we're not taking any chances. We're going to get in and get out with as much as we can carry. We'll make as many trips as we need in the time we have." He pulled out his cell. "Before we move anything, though, I'll take pictures. The investigators will want to create charts showing the debris field."

"What do they hope to determine?"

"What happened."

She looked at the stormy sky. "Didn't lightning strike us?"

"Lightning strikes are common, but they rarely bring a plane down because of the way aircraft are engineered. I can't explain why, at the exact moment we had a strike, the rudder became unresponsive, unless something hit our vertical stabilizer. This could cause the issues we had."

Belle's gaze fixed on him. "What?"

"We may have had a midair collision. This explanation makes more sense to me than a lightning strike bringing us down."

"Is anyone searching for us? Will they find us? Doesn't the plane have some kind of a black box that sends out signals to help them with the search?"

"Yes, though the box is actually orange." He pointed. "Do you see that lone aspen tree between the wreck and our camp?"

She nodded.

"Once I get the pictures, we'll put everything of value under that tree."

Belle hesitated. "What about ..."

He brushed a hand across his forehead, and a muscle moved in his jaw. "We'll have to deal with the bodies later."

All the trips Belle made between the wreck and tree warmed her muscles, but the grimness of their situation chilled her insides. Would anyone come for them? How long must they wait before help arrived? How far from civilization were they? What would they do if they didn't have enough food and water? The high altitude and panic sucked air from her lungs.

"What's wrong, Miss St. John? You're hyperventilating. Calm down." Sutherland dropped his load and grasped her arms. "Listen to me. You're fine. Take a deep breath and hold while I count to ten."

She complied.

"Take another."

Her panic eased. "Will we live, Captain?"

He dropped his hands. "Call me Adam. I hope so. We have a better chance with Colton Morgan."

"Why?"

"He's a rancher and outfitter. He's had a lot of mountain experience."

"What kind of outfitter?" Belle glanced toward Morgan and Liam and took more deep breaths.

"Hunters pay him to pack them and their supplies into the mountains on horses or mules. If they are successful, he brings out their game meat—elk, deer, bear, and moose. He told me he's done this for eighteen years. In the summer, he leases public lands to run his cattle."

Belle watched Morgan. "He doesn't look as old as his bio sounds."

"He's about thirty-three. He told me he started packing hunters at fifteen. I'm glad he's with us."

"I don't think he likes me."

Sutherland cocked an eyebrow. "You just met, so how can you tell?"

Her lips tightened. "I saw the look in his eyes when you introduced us."

The pilot stared.

Belle sighed and faced him fully. "Look at me, Capt—Adam. Describe what you see. Be honest."

Surprise widened his eyes, but he did as she asked. The words he used hinted at admiration and attraction.

Belle nodded. "I watched your face and eyes as you spoke. Your reaction is what I see from most men. This is not the same expression Mr. Morgan wore when he looked at me."

Her nerves calmed. "May I ask what you've done for the last twenty years? Your actions and the way you carry yourself indicate you know what you're doing. You have an air of authority."

He hesitated. "I served as a Navy pilot for many of those years. For the last five, I've flown commercially."

"You were a fighter pilot? You've had survival training?"

"Yes to both questions." He tilted his head toward the others. "Let's get our haul to camp."

Belle breathed easier knowing their chances of living had just increased.

Liam and Morgan helped move the rest of their treasures to the new shelter just before the sky opened and dumped on them.

Belle had never seen such a structure. A pine tree had recently fallen, pulling up a large wall of roots and dirt six inches thick and twenty feet in diameter. The trunk of the fallen giant rested five or more feet off the ground.

Against, and on each side of this natural ridgepole, Morgan and Liam angled many thick branches of similar sizes and interwove them with aspen sapling branches to build an A-frame roughly eight feet long by six feet wide. The dirt wall protected the back of the shelter.

They'd covered the whole thing with several layers of pine and spruce boughs, and they'd piled thick layers of aspen leaves and debris on top of this. Packed soil encircled the base.

On the north side of the A-frame, they'd managed to build an overhang to protect the objects they brought from the plane.

Near the entrance of their shelter, Morgan and Liam had made a small fire pit and edged this with flat stones. A shield of rocks a foot from the fire bounced the heat from the popping flames into the shelter.

Morgan held up a hand. "Before you enter, let's all grab a suitcase from under the overhang and remove any kind of cotton or wool clothing you can find."

They made a dash to the overhang and back to the A-frame.

Morgan pointed. "Liam and I placed several flat stones on the other side of the fire shield. Place the clothing on these rocks."

Belle held up a garment and frowned. "They'll be sopping in a few minutes."

His eyes met hers. "That's the point, Miss St. John. We have no drinking water, so the clothing will catch and hold this for us."

Though Morgan kept his tone neutral, she caught a hint of attitude.

She lifted her chin, straightened her shoulders, and took the pieces of clothing to the stones without a word to him.

Belle knelt and reached for her suitcase. This had been the last find of the day, and her spirits lifted. She unzipped the bag, removed a pair of high heels, and pulled out a red tunic sweater, red mittens, and a matching beanie. She put on another pair of socks and slid black jeans over her leggings. Then she layered the sweater over her now dirty silk blouse and shrugged into her calf-length dress coat before again kneeling in front of her suitcase.

She looked up. Morgan stared at her high heels, one corner of his mouth curled. He lifted his gaze to her face, and their eyes locked. She could almost read his thoughts. Worthless. Dumb blond. Barbie doll.

The hot, acrid taste of resentment filled her mouth, but before she could say anything, he turned away.

"Belle?" Adam Sutherland lowered himself to the bough-covered ground next to her and leaned into her space. He whispered near her ear. "You need to calm down."

Calm down? Who is he to tell me what to do? She turned to him and raised her eyebrows.

"Irritation and dislike are radiating off of you in waves. You need to dampen these feelings if you want to survive. We must work together as a team. We're all each of us has. Understand?"

She studied him for several moments without speaking.

His eyes hardened and his tone firmed. "Belle, I'm serious. Do you understand?"

She snapped a smart salute. "Yes, sir, Captain Sutherland, sir!"

A grin replaced the hard look. "Thank you." He glanced at Morgan, who spoke in low tones with Liam, then returned his gaze to her. "You're probably wrong about him, you know?"

Her lips tightened. “Based on past experience with such people, I don’t think so.”

“Cut him some slack, okay? From what little he’s told me, his life is filled with hard work and interaction with cows, horses, and hunters. He may not be practiced in social graces, especially where women are concerned.”

Belle’s muscles relaxed. “I’ll take this under advisement, Captain.”

He chuckled. “Adam. Please do.”

Belle placed her hand on her growling stomach. “Any idea what we’re going to do for food?”

The pilot looked outside. “The rain is coming down in sheets. We’ll get soaked if we go to the overhang. Let’s check our own bags. I may have a couple of granola bars.”

Morgan and Liam nodded. Both men reached for their backpacks and emptied the contents onto the ground beside them.

Belle removed each item and folded the clothing in a neat stack. Adam did the same.

Liam hooted his triumph and held up four beef jerky sticks and a plastic water bottle. Adam offered his granola bars and two full water bottles, and Morgan added apple wedges, trail mix, and bite-sized chocolate bars to the collection.

Belle brought out her empty metal water bottle, a couple of packages of roasted seaweed snacks, a zipped quart bag of seasoned kale chips, and a bag of grainfree vegetable chips.

When she laid her offering in the mix, the men stared. A smile cracked Adam’s face, and Liam laughed.

Morgan picked up the package and read from the bag. "Organic seaweed, roasted to perfection in olive oil and sprinkled with sea salt." His eyes met hers. "You actually eat this stuff?"

"Of course. Seaweed contains iodine and tyrosine which support thyroid function. The plant is a great source of vitamins and minerals and contains a variety of protective antioxidants. This also provides fiber for good gut health. In all of my parents' five-star restaurants in Dallas, freshly cooked and seasoned seaweed is always offered."

Morgan eyed the bag of dark green kale as if whatever was inside would attack him.

Belle smirked. "The bag of kale chips you are eyeing so distrustfully is full of calcium, iron, potassium, and vitamins A, C, and K. The antioxidants in kale help to protect my cells from free radical damage. We grew this in our garden and baked the leaves in our oven, so I know how fresh the chips are. You should try them before you judge."

No one said anything for a few moments. Neither Adam nor Liam hid their amusement.

Morgan grimaced. "I guess I'm game if you all are."

They divided the food into equal portions. Before anyone could put anything in their mouths, Liam raised to his knees, lifted his eyes, and prayed. "Lord God Almighty, Creator of all things visible and invisible, I thank you for our lives and for the food we now have.

"I also pray for your guidance, protection, and care. Show us what to do. Spare our lives for your sake. In Jesus's holy name I ask these things. Amen."

Belle stared at the young man. He spoke as if talking to God was a regular occurrence and as natural as speaking to anyone else.

She glanced at Morgan and Adam from the corner of her eyes. They, too, looked startled.

Liam lowered himself and sat cross-legged. He smiled when he held up a square of the fragile seaweed. He stuck the whole square in his mouth and chewed. "Not bad."

Belle took a bite of jerky stick and almost gagged. The salt and fat overwhelmed her taste buds. Her eyes watered, but she continued to chew. She slid the rest of the package into her coat pocket and reached for one of Adam's water bottles. She swallowed and washed the taste down before eating an apple wedge.

The jerky didn't sit well in her stomach, so she put the rest of the food in her suitcase.

The rain stopped. She unzipped her cosmetic bag and pulled out her toothbrush, toothpaste, and a sanitizing wipe. She grabbed her empty water bottle and scooted toward the opening. "I'll be right back."

Belle turned on her phone flashlight, grateful the device had survived the crash. She only wished she had service and could call for help. Belle knelt beside the garments she'd placed in the rain and squeezed enough water out of them to fill her water bottle before moving several steps away from the downed pine. She brushed her teeth and relieved herself before using the sanitary wipe.

When she returned to the shelter, the men had spread clothing over the boughs on the ground to act as a sheet.

Someone had placed their suitcases or backpacks at the foot of this pallet.

They left to finish their business, and Belle stared at the small space. Six feet. Four adults. Two men with broad shoulders. Each of them would have fewer than two feet of personal space. Belle sighed. To survive, she would have to share a bed with these strange men. The thought disconcerted her, but she had no other option. She hoped none of them snored.

Belle removed the ear plugs from her cosmetic bag just in case and tied them around her wrist to keep from losing them. She always traveled with the plugs on the off chance she had to sit near a crying child.

The men entered and put their things away. Belle watched their expressions in the glow cast by Adam's phone light and the banked fire. She recognized the moment they realized they would all be bedmates tonight. They looked at each other and then at her.

She returned their stares.

Liam smiled. "I think you should take the middle, Belle. You'll stay warmer."

She nodded, took off her coat to use as a blanket, and scooted to the middle of the pallet.

Morgan tossed each of them an article of clothing. "A pillow for you."

Adam eased into position on her right side, Liam on her left, and Morgan next to him.

Within moments, heat enveloped her. She pulled the coat up to her chin and closed her eyes. She listened to the men's breathing until the sound deepened into the rhythm of sleep.

Night noises intensified in the quietness, and Belle thought she heard the snuffling of some animal. She tensed and raised to her elbows to listen. What if a bear showed up? Their A-frame would provide no protection against such an intruder. She stared at the opening and tried to force her eyes to see beyond the dying firelight. Her breathing turned shallow.

"What's wrong, Belle?" Adam's whispered words held tiredness.

"I think I heard an animal outside."

"They're more afraid of you than you are of them, Miss St. John. Go to sleep." Impatience tinged Morgan's quiet words.

Belle lay down again but couldn't relax.

Adam turned on his side and faced her. He draped an arm across her middle. "You're safe. Rest now."

She took several deep breaths and forced the tenseness out of her muscles. The slight scent of Adam's aftershave comforted her. She sighed. She need not fear with a soldier on one side of her, a man who talked to God on the other, and a mountain man next to him.

Sleep pulled at her.

CHAPTER 2

BELLE'S eyes opened when cold crept under her makeshift blanket. She jerked awake and sat up. Dawn light hinted at another stormy day.

The men were gone, but one of them had tended the fire. For that, she was grateful.

She wanted to go back to sleep, but the cold and her full bladder wouldn't let her.

Belle groaned, removed the coat, and wiggled her way to the end of the pallet. She felt dirty and rumpled from head to toe. She still ached from the crash.

Craning her neck to look outside, she saw no one. In a moment, she had her clothes off and her water bottle, a small bar of hotel soap, and a wipe ready. If she heard anyone approach, she would call out a warning.

Belle muffled a scream when the icy water touched her skin, but she scrubbed harder. She dried with one of the garments they'd used for a bottom sheet.

By the time she heard the men, she'd pulled the red sweater over clean undergarments and a clean base layer, had dabbed a drop of perfume behind each ear, and worked to brush the snarls out of her long hair.

Morgan stooped to enter but stopped and stared. His nostrils flared, and his eyes widened.

"Good morning." Belle smiled and remembered her promise to give this man—her teammate—a chance.

Liam bumped into Morgan. "What's wrong?"

Without a word, the outfitter ducked inside and made room for the others.

They, too, stopped and stared before sitting.

Adam smiled. "You look ready to start the day, Belle." He grimaced and looked at the other two. "Probably better than we look at the moment."

Belle noted the dark stubble on Adam's and Morgan's jaws and their rumpled clothes. Liam looked much the same as he had yesterday.

She nodded and worked her way to the entrance. "If you'll excuse me, I have business to take care of."

When she returned, they sat cross-legged with what remained of their food from last night.

Belle retrieved hers and waited. As one, she, Adam, and Morgan turned to Liam.

He smiled and again offered a prayer of thanksgiving and a request for mercy.

Belle decided to leave the jerky stick as a last resort. She ate the remainder of her seaweed snacks, her portion of the trail mix, and one chocolate bite. Once they ran out, she didn't know what they would do.

"We need to take care of the bodies today, Belle." Adam hesitated. "Do you want to help or do something else?"

Belle shuddered. "Do something else."

He nodded.

Morgan held a kale chip to the light and spoke without looking at her. "You can go through the suitcases under the overhang to see what we have."

His comment didn't set well with Belle. She knew this needed to be done and knew he only stated fact, but something about going through dead people's things seemed sacrilegious.

"Liam, if I do this, will I be committing a sin or be doing something I shouldn't?"

Morgan snorted, but Liam seemed to take her question seriously. "Belle, when God called these people to their appointments with him, they left immediately, with no thought to the material things they left behind.

"When David, the shepherd who became king of Israel, and his soldiers ate some bread only the priests were allowed to eat, God did not condemn them. They were hungry and needed food.

"We will not be sinning if we use the things they left behind to survive."

Adam nodded. "I'll take pictures of the bodies with whatever jewelry they have on and will put these possessions in the plastic bag you had the kale in. If we get out of here, I'll return these to their people."

If we get out of here, not when ... Belle's stomach lurched. "Okay, I'll go through the bags."

The men left, and Belle walked around the A-frame to the north and stared at the luggage eight dead people left behind. She didn't know if they'd found everything, but these pieces were closest to the wreck.

She put her hands on her hips and tried to determine where she would put the sorted objects. If she laid flat rocks in the space between the A-frame and the overhang, she'd have a relatively clean surface to place items. This she did.

Belle reached for the first suitcase and took a deep breath before unzipping the co-pilot's case. She looked toward the crash and wondered how Adam was dealing with the death of his friend.

By the time the men returned in the afternoon, grim faced and dirty, she had sorted all the items.

"Come. See what we have." She signaled for them to follow her.

They stared at her neat groupings of clothing, cosmetic products, edibles, and miscellaneous items. She'd left the cases open so she could zip them and store the clothing out of the weather.

"Well done, Belle." Adam's tired voice and drawn expression told her how unpleasant their task had been.

"Where did you put them?"

Adam rubbed his forehead. "We laid them side-by-side next to the fuselage and covered them with brush to keep the birds away. I'm glad the weather held."

Morgan had found his rifle case and some other objects. He laid these on the ground and tilted his head toward Liam. "The Preacher said words over them and sang. He's good."

Liam nodded and gave her a tired grin. "I told Mr. Morgan I wasn't a preacher, only a praise and worship leader."

Morgan knelt and unlocked the case. "Didn't matter to them or us, Liam." The outfitter smiled when he stared at the contents. "Everything is here, and nothing seems to be damaged, but I'll have to resight." He lifted a hunting knife and hatchet and examined their surfaces. He unbuckled his belt, attached the knife and hatchet cases, and relooped and buckled.

Belle stared at Morgan's expression. When he slid the blades into their cases and lifted the rifle, the lines at the side of his eyes eased, and he sighed as if in relief—like he hadn't been fully dressed until now.

She turned to the pilot. "When do you think the searchers might come? Shouldn't they find us soon?"

He looked into the threatening sky. Lightning lit up the clouds. "I don't know. Air traffic control diverted me around the storm, so they know we're in the general area. The search process will start as soon as our crash has been reported."

She studied his face. "But? I get the sense you aren't telling me something."

He sighed. "Many things can delay a rescue, Belle, weather being one of them. We're in the middle of September just below timberline. Snow can fall at any time here. Who knows what distance rescuers have to cover to get to us? The terrain may make access impossible except by helicopter."

Belle eyed the small amount of food she'd salvaged from the cases. "So, we may be here a few more days?"

She caught the look that passed between Adam and Morgan, and her insides trembled. *They think we'll be here longer than a few days.*

Breathe! she commanded her lungs.

Adam reached for their empty plastic water bottles. "At least we have a water source now. We found a clear stream flowing out of rocks not too far from here. I'll fill these before the rain hits."

Belle slung on her coat and grabbed a washcloth, a small bar of soap, and a hand towel she'd found in the luggage. "I'll go with you."

They walked to the spring without speaking. When they got there, Adam filled the bottles, and Belle washed her face and hands. She rinsed and then held the cold, wet cloth to the bruise on her cheek. She still ached from the crash, and sudden movements reminded her of her recent impact with the ground.

She handed the washcloth and soap to Adam.

The pilot grinned. "Hard to sleep next to a bedmate who stinks, right?" He removed his uniform jacket and dress shirt and handed them to her before splashing the icy water on his muscular chest and under his arms.

Belle watched him lather and rinse. "Tell me the truth. How long can we survive if rescuers don't find us within the next few days?"

He dried. "I can't answer that, Belle. I don't know. Too many variables are in play here. Our odds of staying alive will decrease once snow falls."

"What about Morgan's rifle? Can't he shoot something?"

"I don't think the game animals will come near the smell of jet fuel and humans."

She handed him his jacket and shirt.

He slung on the jacket but left off the shirt. "I'd better try to find something else to wear. Even I can smell the ripeness."

Morgan and Liam looked up when they returned.

Liam took the water bottles Belle handed him while Adam reached inside his suitcase for a clean shirt.

Morgan tilted his head toward a small pile of food for each of them. "After tonight, we need to limit our food intake to once a day."

Belle stared at her ration. Did hers contain an item or two more than the others?

Liam asked the blessing, and they sat in silence and munched on whatever had been placed in front of them.

Belle brushed the crumbs off her hands and turned to Adam. "The rain has started, so I think this is a good time for a story. Tell us about yourself."

He shook his head. "My story isn't interesting, Belle, but if you want to hear, I'll give you the shortened version. I enlisted in the Navy a year after high school. During that time, I married my high school sweetheart. I remained in the Navy until I got news she had a fast-spreading cancer. She died five years ago, and I switched careers. End of story."

"I'm sorry to hear about your wife, Adam. What was her name?"

"Debbie."

No one said anything for several moments, until Liam cleared his throat. "Are your parents still alive? Do you have siblings?"

The pilot nodded. "My parents are alive, and I have two sisters—one older and one younger. They are married and have two children each. My wife and I always wanted children, but this didn't work out."

Adam turned to her. "What's your story, Belle? I'm sure yours is more interesting than mine."

"I'm twenty-five and the only child of parents who own several five-star restaurants in Dallas. From an early age, I traveled with them to Europe to meet with suppliers. I grew to love the people and the varied dishes from different countries, but all this international travel created hard times for me in public school."

She didn't want to continue, but Liam looked as if he would ask a question. Morgan stared at her with a strange expression.

"Kids at school picked on me and called me *spoiled rich girl*, and the girls turned mean when I started to attract their boyfriends' attention." She grimaced. "I wasn't interested in their boyfriends, and I wasn't spoiled. My parents raised me to be grateful for what we have and to not look down on others who don't have as much. Several days each year, we work in soup kitchens and homeless shelters to keep ourselves grounded in reality, and our restaurants provide the Thanksgiving and Christmas meals in several parts of the city. Mom and Dad work an excessive number of hours to get where they are, and they expect me to work as hard.

"I got tired of all the lies and bullying and asked my parents to let me do a study abroad program to finish out my senior year. I spent that year in Madrid, Spain, gaining fluency in the language.

"The next year, I went to a cordon bleu school in Paris to expand the knowledge I'd gained in my parents' restaurants. I love to cook and to see people enjoying what I've made. I have from a young age."

Adam watched her face. "You speak French?"

She nodded, "Spanish, French, and Italian."

Liam straightened. "*Hablo español también. Viví en América del Sur la mayor parte de mi vida.*"

Belle stared at the younger man, her eyebrows raised, and repeated what he said in English. "You speak Spanish because you lived in South America for most of your life?"

He nodded and answered in English. "My parents were missionaries. I've lived in Argentina, Bolivia, Chile, and Uruguay."

Adam studied her face. "Do you have a boyfriend or husband?"

She grimaced. "No. Finding a man who is interested in me instead of my parents' money is much harder than I expected. I want a home and family with a man who loves me for who I am and who doesn't care how much money I have, but this dream seems to be out of my reach."

Morgan watched her face. "If you find this man, would you expect to live in Dallas near your folks?"

She shrugged. "Not necessarily. I'm flexible. We have a horse ranch east of the city. I spent many summers there learning to ride and enjoying the open spaces. I visit when I want to avoid the rat race of the city. I love the country too."

The muscles in Morgan's jaws moved. He looked as if he would ask something else but changed his mind. The intent look in his eyes gave her pause.

"Colton, why were you on the flight?" At Adam's words, they turned to Morgan.

"I'd been hunting whitetail deer in Louisiana. I told one of my clients I would meet him in Phoenix to attend a large gun show. We planned to return to Montana together for the start of the hunting season. Guess our plans have changed."

Adam raised a brow. "Belle, what were you doing on a flight from Denver to Phoenix if you live in Dallas?"

"I was in Denver on business. I intended to meet a friend in Phoenix. We were going to spend several days together before she returned to Oregon."

Adam nodded and turned to Liam. "And you?"

"To lead the morning and evening worship and praise services for a Christian writers' conference this weekend."

Belle stared. "How many people attend such a conference?"

"About seven hundred."

Belle shuddered. "I'd be terrified to stand up in front of that many people."

Liam smiled. "But you've never heard the beauty of seven hundred voices worshipping in unison in a large auditorium. I am sure, once they hear of the crash, all of them will be praying for us."

Her eyes met Liam's. "Sing. Sing what you would've sung there."

Without hesitation, Liam sang. The words flowed as if they came from the depths of his soul. She closed her eyes. She could listen to his exceptional voice for hours.

When night came, they lay side-by-side in the A-frame and listened to the whipping wind and the booming thunder.

Belle spoke her thoughts. "If the searchers don't find us tomorrow or the next day, what will we do?"

Morgan answered, his voice quiet. “We need to start looking for signs humans have been here. If they have, they will use trails that can take us back to civilization. We can’t stay here. If we do, this will become our tomb. I can smell and feel a change in the air. We’ll get snow soon.”

Belle thought her heart would pound out of her chest.

Liam turned toward Morgan. “What kind of signs?”

“Initials and dates carved into tree trunks, blazes indicating direction, orange tape on brush, or deadfall someone cut with a chainsaw to allow easier passage for horses or mules. Colorado archery and muzzleloader seasons have started, so we listen for shooting. We watch for hunters in camouflage and bright orange vests. We watch for mule or horse tracks or droppings.”

Belle forced herself to take deep breaths. Easy for him to know what to look for. “Snow in September?”

“I’ve been in the Rocky Mountains in September looking for cows, Miss St. John. I had to hole up for two days because the snow piled up to a foot.”

She swallowed the lump in her throat. “Your life sounds beyond difficult, Mr. Morgan.”

“I don’t know about that. Some days are hard, some days are easy, but this is the only life I know. I can’t think of anything else I’d rather do.” His eyes met and held hers. He seemed to be trying to convey a message beyond his words—a message she didn’t understand.

Morgan remained silent for several moments. “We can pair up and work in widening circles from our camp.”

The next morning, Belle and Adam headed east, while Morgan and Liam turned to the southeast.

They'd made plans to search for three hours before returning to camp to share what they had found. They filled every water bottle and divided these among themselves.

Belle looked around as she followed Adam. "How will we know how to get back to camp?"

"We pay attention to landmarks and the location of the sun, now that we can see the sun, and we mark our trail. As we move farther from camp, I'll hang these red cloth strips on branches on my right. To return, we'll keep the markers on our left."

Belle's fears at being in such an alien environment eased as she followed a couple of steps behind him.

When she was a pre-teen, she dreamed she was in the driver's seat of her parents' car when the vehicle started rolling backward down the drive. The car picked up speed, and she didn't know what to do. She believed she would be killed if the car rolled into the street and another driver hit her. Even now she recalled the panic.

After several nights of the same frightening dream, she shared her fears with her dad.

"All you have to do is push on the brake and set the hand brake."

Those few words banished the nightmares after she envisioned herself going through the actions. Adam's explanation gave her the same feeling.

Every now and then, he would point and say, "This place would make a good shelter."

Belle studied his face. "How do you know so much?"

He shrugged. "Certain types of soldiers are sent to SERE training school. I was one of them."

"What is that?"

"The letters stand for Survival, Evasion, Resistance, and Escape. Only those of us who have a high chance of being shot down or captured in enemy territory are given this training."

"Like?"

"Fighter pilots and special forces."

"Sounds difficult."

"Brutal is a better word, Belle. SERE school is the most feared type of military training."

"What did you have to do?"

His eyes scanned the vegetation. "After our orientation course, we had almost six months of training in tactics to survive in forest, desert, coastal, tropic, and open ocean environments. We were expected to become expert in personnel recovery, first aid, rough land evacuation, and hand-to-hand combat."

He stopped and pointed. "Look. Oak brush. Let's gather as many acorns as we can to take back with us."

They didn't have any containers, so Belle lifted her long sweater to form a basket, and Adam harvested several pounds of acorns.

She didn't ask if they were edible. After hearing about his training, she figured he knew what he was doing and followed him back to camp.

CHAPTER 3

BELLE dumped the acorns onto the stone floor behind the fire shield and reached for one of them. Hunger was her constant companion now.

Liam and Morgan returned to camp, their arms full of wood, just as she was about to pop one into her mouth.

Morgan shook his head. "Don't eat that, Miss St. John, or you'll be sorry."

She frowned. "Adam says they're edible."

Morgan nodded and unloaded his armful of wood near the fire stones. "They are, but you have to shell them. To get rid of the bitterness, you need to soak them in warm water for at least twelve hours."

Twelve hours? She was hungry now.

Liam dropped his load and brushed the dirt from his hands. "I can heat some water in your bottle, Belle, if you want to soak some."

Morgan reached in his pocket and pulled out fresh pine needles. "Put these in the metal bottle instead. We'll have tea."

Belle eyed her harvest. "But what about the acorns?"

"Break the shells and dig the meat out. While you and Liam do this, I'll make another heating container."

Adam returned from the spring just as they started the tedious process of shelling using flat rocks. He joined them.

As she shelled, Belle watched as Morgan used his hunting knife to cut a couple of inches off the top of one of the plastic bottles. He punched two holes opposite each other and about a half-inch down then stood.

Without saying anything, he moved to the back of their fallen tree and pulled away several long strands of root now exposed to the air. He divided the strands in half with his fingers and poked one end through the holes he'd made in the plastic. These strands created a hanger of some sort.

Then he made a tripod out of similar-sized branches and tied these together with the root ball cordage.

Liam stared. "Won't the bottle melt?"

Colton shook his head. "We'll let the fire die down and we'll hang this over the coals. As long as we have water in the bottle, the bottle won't melt."

Belle wondered at the man's skill. "How do you know all this?"

One corner of his mouth curled up. "I graduated from the school of hard knocks, Miss St. John, but sometimes, I watched internet videos."

They ate the last of the rations and drank the pine needle tea before crawling inside their shelter. Belle's stomach grumbled. She longed to taste the acorns, but Colton said to let them soak overnight.

She sighed. When would help come?

Belle followed three steps behind Morgan. They searched for water and a way out. The outfitter moved with grace and in near silence. He never seemed to step on dead branches or stumble over rocks like she did, even carrying the rifle, and her chagrin mounted. She tried to copy his movements and to step where he stepped. This helped, but she would never come close to his ability.

His head constantly turned as he studied everything in his surroundings.

"Why do you dislike me so much?" Had the words she'd been thinking actually left her mouth?

Morgan jerked to a stop and stiffened as if she'd hit him in the back with something. Slowly, he faced her. "What makes you think I don't like you?"

Belle snorted. "Everything." She could not interpret the expression in his eyes. "I saw the dismissive look you gave me when we were first introduced. Your lips curled sarcastically when you gazed at my high heels. I've picked up on attitude in almost every one of our interactions. I know you think I'm useless and not very smart, because I've seen such looks and heard the words since I was a teen. However, I don't know what I've done to make you despise me."

Morgan's voice roughened. "You actually believe this?"

"Of course. What else should I think?"

His green eyes blazed and his body tensed. "The first time I saw you on the plane, I felt like a bronc kicked me in the gut. I couldn't take my eyes off of you. I thought you were the most beautiful person I'd seen.

You had a kind face and no wedding band. I watched your expressions and listened to you chat with the woman across the aisle the whole flight. You stirred up a hornet's nest of emotions in me. I still felt these when the pilot introduced us. I didn't want you to see."

He ran his fingers through his hair. "You were the first person I looked for after we crashed.

"And the shoes? I imagined how you'd look in the dress that goes with them, and how I would look if I asked you to dance. Not a pretty picture."

He laughed without humor. "You make me crazy, Belle. Do you know what torture I endure knowing the pilot sleeps on one side of you and the preacher on the other? They enjoy your warmth and scent every night, and I'm left on the outside with a jealous knot twisting my insides."

Belle's mouth dropped and her eyes widened. Her heart raced. How could she have so thoroughly misjudged this man?

"Mr. Morgan, I—"

"My name is Colton." He stepped into her space, buried his hands in the hair on each side of her face, and covered her mouth with his. The intensity and passion of his kiss burned to her toes and stirred an emotion she didn't recognize. He smelled like pine trees, cold, and mountains.

Colton lifted his head only to lower his lips to trail a string of warm kisses down her neck.

She raised a tentative hand to his bearded cheek and stared at him, not knowing how or if she should respond.

He groaned and stepped back. "I should not have done that. As much as I'd like to think all things are possible, I'm a realist. No one needs to tell me we don't make sense together, Belle. You and the pilot or even the preacher make better sense than you and I do. We live in two different worlds, so forgive my lack of control."

"You barely know me, Colton. How can you feel so strongly—?"

"For the last four days, we've spent twenty-four hours a day together. I watch and listen to you. You're a city girl, but I haven't heard you complain. That tells me you're tougher than I expected. You do your part to the best of your abilities. I admire that."

He waited for her to process his words.

"Do you think rescuers will ever find us?"

He looked at the building clouds. "The longer we stay here, the less likely they will find us alive, which is why we have to help ourselves. I'm glad the pilot is with us. He's highly skilled."

She nodded. "He says the same about you."

Colton turned and continued his search. Something caught his attention and his stride lengthened. She had a hard time keeping up. In her haste, she tripped over a partially covered limb.

She cried out as she fell into a jumbled mess of dead branches. Her left knee hit a rock, and a sharp, broken stob jammed itself into the meat on the inside of her left shin. The warmth and wetness of blood panicked her.

Belle called out, but the outfitter was not in sight. Tears flowed as she struggled to rise, and pain sucked the breath out of her lungs. Fear curdled her blood. As far as she knew, they were hundreds of miles from any hospital.

She took a step in the direction she'd seen him go, but the pain was too much. Instead, she lowered herself to the ground and clamped her right hand over the wound. She wept. Surely, Morgan would realize he'd lost her and would return. She didn't know how long she stayed in that position.

"Belle?" Colton rushed to her, removed the rifle from his shoulder, and knelt. "What happened? I looked around and you weren't behind me. I worried you'd gotten off on the wrong trail."

"I fell." Blood dripped between the fingers of her right hand.

Colton's breath hissed between his teeth. "Oh, sweetheart. Hang on."

He removed his shirt and T-shirt. With a smooth movement, he slid the knife from the case and cut bandage-width strips out of the material before returning the knife to his belt.

"We'll look at this when we get back to camp." He wrapped the bandage around her leg before replacing his shirt. He helped her to her feet, slung the rifle to his left shoulder, and hugged her to his right side. "Put your arm around my neck and lean on me. Let's get you back to camp."

Belle didn't realize hopping on one leg could be so exhausting. The distance to camp seemed much longer than the distance they'd walked away from camp. They stopped often, but Colton gave no sign of impatience. She was grateful.

Adam and Liam rushed to meet them, concern on their faces.

"What happened?" Adam slung Belle's other arm around his neck, and he and Colton carried her.

"I tripped."

Liam tilted his head toward the fire. "I have hot water. I heated this in the metal water bottle. I'll get the soap and a cloth."

Colton kept his eyes on her. "Liam, bring Belle's bottle of hand sanitizer and those packets of honey she found in one of the suitcases."

They laid her on the ground in front of the fire. Her kneecap hurt so much, she groaned.

"We're going to have to remove the pant leg to just above your knee, Belle." Adam waited for her nod before cutting away the bloody fabric. He threw the mess into the fire.

Slowly, they studied her leg.

Belle watched each man's face to see what they truly thought of the wound, but their expressions were focused and showed little emotion.

Adam looked up. "Your knee is bruised and swelling. I don't know if you cracked the bone or damaged the soft tissue."

Liam returned with the sanitizer and honey. He handed Adam the hot, wet cloth.

Adam cleaned the puncture and long scratch as gently as he could then asked for the sanitizer.

Liam popped the cap and gave him the bottle.

The pilot stroked her cheek. "This is going to hurt, but we have to sanitize the wounds. Are you ready?"

Belle nodded and cried out the moment he squeezed the sanitizer into the hole. She gritted her teeth and scrunched her eyes closed, but these actions didn't stop the tears that squeezed out of the corners or the groans.

"Hang on, Belle." Colton clasped her hand.

She squeezed hard to keep from screaming.

"Done." Adam dabbed the wound.

Belle opened her eyes. Her leg stung as if she'd been bitten by a hive of angry bees.

Colton told Liam to open the honey packets and give them to Adam.

He did, but raised his eyebrows. "Why honey?"

Colton looked at Belle as if she had asked the question. "I grew up on a cattle ranch in Montana. Doctors were not close, so if we got cut, my mom would clean the cut then open a jar of fresh honey and dab this on the wound. The cuts never got infected, and the honey gave me a little pain relief.

"She also made my brothers and me eat a teaspoon of raw honey every day during the blooming season to keep allergies at bay. Honey is the only thing I know that will never spoil."

Belle stared at him, her hand still grasping his. "Are your parents and siblings still alive?"

He nodded. "They all live on the ranch. My brothers and their wives built near the folks."

"You like having family so close?"

"Yes. Though they're my brothers, we're good friends. We help each other when help is needed. We get together at Mom and Dad's for Thanksgiving and Christmas. The place feels alive with the children running around and laughing. We can smell the good food from the time we step inside the door."

Belle imagined the joy and laughter. As an only child with a small extended family, she had not experienced the fun of a large one, though her holidays were always pleasant and spent with her parents.

Could he see the wistfulness in her eyes? She lowered her lashes.

They bound up her wound with more of the T-shirt bandages and helped her sit up.

Adam shook his head. "We don't have any pain medicine, Belle. I'm sorry. I suspect you're going to have a rough time."

Colton straightened and reached for his rifle. He slung the weapon over his shoulder and turned to Adam. "I found something. We need to head back out while we still have daylight."

He glanced at Belle. "You'll be okay while we're gone?"

She nodded.

Liam patted Belle's hand. "I'll stay with her."

The pilot and outfitter left, and Belle studied Liam's face. "Thank you."

"You're welcome. What can I do for you?"

Her deepest fears voiced themselves. "You can pray searchers will find us while we're still alive, that my injury won't get infected, and that we'll get food soon."

Without hesitation, he lifted his requests to God. Not only did he pray for her, Adam, and Colton, but he prayed for their families and the searchers. His words comforted her.

"Liam, why would God let this happen? Does he want to punish us for something?"

"God doesn't work that way, Belle."

"Then why did this happen?"

He shrugged. "God's ways and thoughts are much higher than ours. He loves us and wants the best for us."

Belle looked around. "His best is for us to crash and be stranded in the woods?"

Liam looked into the sky, then at her. "His will is for you to know him. To know his loving kindness, mercy, and power. To be reconciled to him. How he does this is his choice. Maybe he knew you would not consider him in your busy life, so he isolated you so you could focus."

"But why would he allow you to be in the same situation? Do you need to focus?"

He smiled. "My guess is he put me here for you, Adam, and Colton. I gave my life to him a long time ago, and he's always been faithful.

"Look around, Belle. All creation speaks of his majesty and greatness. He says he has written the knowledge of who he is in the heavens and in our hearts, and he has revealed himself in his word, the Bible."

His words pierced her. She believed in God, but he had not played a major role in her life. She and her parents belonged to a church, but they went only when they had time or on Easter and Christmas.

"Sing to me, Liam."

The songs again flowed from him. Though he sang for her, he sang to his God. When he added sticks to the fire to keep the water container hot or to add more acorns, he sang. He sang when he stripped pine boughs from the nearby trees and added them to the bed. She didn't know so many songs of praise had been written.

The other two returned with only an hour left of daylight.

Belle sat with a cold pack on her knee. Liam had made the pack out of her kale and veggie chip bags. He'd put one bag inside the other, filled this pack with the icy water from the creek, then zipped them shut. When the water warmed, he replaced this with the cold. Her knee didn't hurt as much.

Adam carried a bucket like those that came from one of the DIY home stores, and Colton carried a metal quart pot without a handle and two long, forked sticks.

Her eyes widened. They'd found signs of people? Her heartbeat picked up.

Adam looked at her cold pack and nodded. "How do you feel?"

"Okay. The pain is tolerable."

He nodded. "Good. I'm going to the spring to fill the bucket. Liam, will you come with the pot Colton brought?"

"Sure." He stood and reached for the container.

Colton bent and offered a hand. "Belle, stand up. I want to measure these sticks. You'll have crutches soon."

He measured, cut the thick sticks to size, then started wrapping the forks with a shirt he'd taken from the articles of clothing and cut into three-inch strips.

"Try them." He held them out.

She put the crutches under her arms and hobbled around. "They'll work. Thanks."

Their eyes met. He started to say something, but Liam and Adam returned.

Adam sat the bucket down and went for the last peanut butter cup they had. He knelt in front of the partially filled container and smeared the thick sweetness in the middle of a wooden dowel someone had placed in larger holes on each side of the bucket.

"What are you doing?" His actions distracted her from her aches and pains.

He didn't look up from his work. "Making a trap. We need protein. We'll leave this bucket outside tonight and see what we catch in the morning."

Belle couldn't guess what kind of animals they intended to trap, but she hoped they were successful. Hunger nagged at her.

She stared at the large pile of shelled and leached acorns, then looked at Colton. "Are we able to eat these now?"

He nodded and grinned. "Yes. Enjoy."

They divided the food and again turned to Liam. He prayed, and as soon as Belle heard amen, she put several nuts in her mouth.

Ah, the delight of chewing! Her stomach demanded more, now, but she deliberately ate as slowly as she could to savor the feeling of food in her mouth and stomach. She ate the rest of her portion one nut at a time.

She followed her meal with pine needle tea Liam had made in the quart-sized pot he'd filled.

Colton sniffed the air. "We need to move camp tomorrow."

Belle stared at his face. “Move camp? Why? Where?” Did he hear the disquiet in her tone?

He looked into the dark sky. “The weather is changing. I can smell and feel this change. We need to get to a lower altitude. Adam and I found a hunters’ camp about a mile away and several hundred feet lower in elevation. They left some things behind we can use.”

“What kind of things?”

“Pots, pans, eating utensils, a couple of shovels, some other things—things they didn’t want to haul out because they’d have to pack them back in the next year.”

“Will they return to their camp soon? Can we just wait there for them and ask them to take us out?”

Colton’s eyes met Adam’s before he looked at her. “We don’t know if they’ll return this year, Belle. No one has been there for a while, and this is the start of the muzzleloader season. The archery season started two weeks ago, so they don’t seem to be archers or black powder hunters. If they do come, they may be hunting during one of the late rifle seasons in October. We can’t wait that long for them.”

Belle’s spirits lifted, yet at the same time, the thought of leaving this shelter and moving away from the crash site bothered her. If they moved, wouldn’t the searchers have more difficulty finding them?

In bed that night, she listened to their breathing. None of them slept. “How will the rescuers know where we’ve gone?”

Adam turned over and put an arm across her middle. “We’ll use the empty suitcases to make an arrow near the crash site. This will show them the direction we’ve gone. Then we'll mark our trail. They'll have trackers who know what to look for."

Belle's worry calmed. She turned on her side to face him. "I'm glad you're here and not dead."

He caressed her face and kissed her forehead. "I am too. Now get some sleep."

CHAPTER 4

COLD woke Belle. Her knee and calf ached unbearably, and she felt dirty from head to toe. If those weren't bad enough, her empty stomach complained loudly.

When she struggled from the shelter, the men looked up. They stood around the fire in their coats.

"I'm sorry."

Adam raised his brows. "Why are you sorry, Belle?"

"I know I tossed and groaned all night, and none of you got much sleep because of me."

He shrugged. "We expected this. No need to apologize."

Liam handed her the crutches. "I filled your pack with cold water."

She shivered. The missing pant leg let in too much cold under her dress coat. She needed to put her leggings back on, but how would she care for the wound then?

Belle grimaced. She must look ridiculous.

Her stomach grumbled, and she glanced toward the bucket. "What did we catch? I heard splashing all night."

Colton shrugged. "Come and see."

Belle hobbled over, looked in the bucket, and gagged.

Mice. Many of them.

She shuddered, and her eyes moved from Colton's face to Adam's and back. "You're serious?"

Colton nodded. "We'll take them with us to the next camp. We can pan fry them there. Let's pack up."

Adam handed her a backpack from their stash. "Put whatever you want inside this. We'll need to use your suitcase. Liam? Ready?"

"Yes." Liam picked up two pieces of luggage in each hand and started toward the crash site.

Adam and Colton followed with more.

Belle glanced at the bucket several times as she packed. Her stomach roiled.

She sat and placed the cold pack on her kneecap and looked at the sky. Clouds built, and even she, city girl that she was, could sense a difference in the weather. "Please," she whispered. "Help us get out of here."

The men made one more trip then returned.

Colton squatted next to her. "Let's take a look at the wound." He unwound the bandage, and the three studied her injury.

Adam looked up. "Did you pack the sanitizer?"

"Yes." She scooted the backpack toward him. "In the outside zipper pocket."

The sanitizer didn't sting as much.

Colton studied the wound. "I can't see any sign of infection. Let's get you wrapped up again." He looked at the sky. "We'll have only a few hours to get camp set up."

Belle drank the pine needle tea Liam handed her.

Colton checked to make sure all the things they might need to survive had been packed, and any unnecessary things were piled together at the entrance to their shelter. He stared at the high heels she'd left. His lips tightened.

Belle couldn't read the expression in his eyes to interpret his thoughts.

Colton put on his backpack, then slung the rifle to his shoulder. Without a word, he turned toward the southeast.

Belle again marveled at how graceful the man was in the woods and how natural he looked with a pack and rifle.

Liam followed with his backpack, and Adam indicated she should go in front of him. He strapped on his pack and picked up the mouse bucket. "I'll help you if you need me to, and I'll make sure you don't get off the trail."

"Thanks." Belle hobbled as fast as she could on the crude crutches. Learning to use them efficiently took her a half hour and, by that time, she knew her underarms would be sore by the time they reached camp.

She firmed her jaw and tightened her lips. She would not complain, especially after Colton's words. But as she followed, the only thing she could think of was having to eat mice soon.

People in Africa and Asia eat mice and rats all the time. Some think they are delicacies.

"I know," she whispered to herself, "but I'm not in Africa or Asia."

You're not in your five-star restaurant either.

"Belle, are you okay?" Adam came up beside her.

She unclenched her teeth. "I'm okay."

He studied her face. "You're pale. Do you need to rest?"

"How much farther?"

He pointed. "About three hundred yards in those trees."

"I'm okay. Let's just get there so I can get off these crutches."

"Have a drink first." He sat the bucket down and offered his water bottle.

She drank. "Thanks."

Colton wasted no time. By the time Belle got there, he and Liam had started a fire and set a cast iron skillet to heat on a grill the hunters had left, then he pulled out his hatchet and chopped limbs of similar sizes nearby.

"Here, Belle." Liam placed a stump near the fire. "Sit."

She did and looked around. Whoever had been here left a ridgepole mounted between two aspen trees. The space under this was larger than their previous shelter and was high enough a person could enter standing. "How many hunters use this camp?"

Colton dropped a load of cut branches nearby. "About four or five."

Belle watched as the men pulled logs away from a hole in the ground to reveal large black plastic bags filled with something.

Liam dumped the contents of a bag onto the ground. A tarp. "We won't get wet now, Belle."

The men draped the tarp over the ridgepole and attached the base ropes to stakes already in the ground before angling the cut limbs to rest on the pole outside the tarp, much like Colton had done earlier.

With three men harvesting pine boughs, their shelter and the floor inside were soon covered with thick layers of protection.

Belle stood and limped to the large hole in the ground and pulled out another trash bag. She reached inside and held up a small bottle of olive oil and salt and pepper shakers. She stared. Of all the mountains where they could have crashed, they landed on one people had used. People who left important things behind.

She looked into the cloudy sky. Had this been God's doing? Had he led them to the things they most needed to stay alive? Why did he allow them to live but not the others on the plane? Did he have a plan, or was all of this just a series of random events?

Colton pointed toward his left. "You can set up the kitchen there."

She eyed the homemade counter. The hunters had cut branches of the same length and attached them to the outside of two aspen trees standing about four feet apart. Across these, they'd laid slats of split pine to form a crude but effective surface.

Belle placed the olive oil and salt and pepper shakers on this, then returned to the bag to look for other treasures. Seasoned salt, two cans of green beans, one of refried beans, and a can opener soon joined them. She found metal plates, silverware, and cups and placed them on the makeshift counter.

The men stooped over the bucket and reached for the drowned mice. They skinned, gutted, and removed heads, tails, and feet. Bile rose, and she turned away.

Colton stopped beside her. "Will you cook, Belle? I'm sure you'll be better than any of us. I'll bring the oil, you bring the seasoning. The skillet is clean and hot."

She stared at the pile of chunked mice meat and covered her mouth. "I don't think I can do this."

Colton nodded. "Sure, you can. We need animal protein, and this is all we have."

Belle searched each of their hopeful faces. "All right. Hand me the oil."

She simmered the meat in the oil, then added seasoning. Her stomach demanded food the moment her nose caught a whiff of the frying meat.

When she handed them each a plateful, they smiled and waited for Liam to pray.

Belle stared at her full plate. The revulsion in her mind fought against the hunger in her belly.

Liam touched her shoulder. "My parents lived in Argentina in 1972, when a flight from Montevideo, Uruguay, crashed in the Andes in October near the border between Argentina and Chile. The plane carried a rugby team, their families and supporters, and crew members.

"My folks told me forty-five passengers and crew were on the flight. Several died immediately on impact, several more died soon after from severe injuries and frigid temperatures. They were stranded for seventy-two days and faced exposure, avalanches, and starvation."

Belle blanched. "Seventy-two days? Did any survive?"

Liam nodded. “Sixteen of them. Two walked out. They found help, but do you know how the people stayed alive?”

“They ate mice?”

“No. They cannibalized the dead.” He waited for his words to sink in. “Eating mice is a better option, don’t you think?”

Without a word, she put a bite in her mouth.

For the next half hour, they focused only on the meal before them. They spat out bones with each bite.

Belle stared at her empty plate, stunned that she wished for more.

Adam chuckled. “What are you thinking, Belle? The look on your face is priceless.”

She looked up. “I’m thinking this dish will never make the menu at our restaurants, but if my options are to eat a mouse or one of you, I’ll take the mouse.”

Belle eyed each of them. “I think you all would be too tough and stringy to eat.”

Colton laughed. The sound came from deep in his belly. “Did you just make a joke, Belle?”

She stared at him. “I don’t think so. Just stating facts.”

Her answer made the men laugh.

Colton stood. “We need to find their water source.”

Liam brushed off his clothes. “I’ll help you look.”

Adam and Colton lifted the rest of the bags out of the storage hole.

Belle watched. “Why did they bury their stuff?”

Colton pulled away an old rubber blow-up mattress used as a covering and reached for a couple of containers that looked like flattened plastic gas cans. "To keep bears and other critters out of their things."

"Bears?" Wide-eyed, Belle surveyed the trees around them.

He turned to look at her. "Yes. I found fresh bear scat a few hundred yards from here. Looks like they're stocking up on acorns and chokecherries."

Adam reached for two more water containers. "How far do you think we'll have to go to find the hunters' water source?"

Colton fisted his hands on his hips and looked around. "Probably a few hundred yards."

The men set out in different directions, and Belle wished one had stayed behind to go with her to the oak patch to collect acorns.

A sharp whistle indicated one of the men had found the water. Thirty minutes later, they returned carrying four full jugs. Liam had harvested several pounds of acorns and dumped these on the ground beside the fire.

Belle lowered herself from the stump to the ground, picked up a rock, and started shelling.

"Thanks, Belle. I'll start the water heating." Liam brought the biggest pot he could find and offered this to Colton to fill before placing the pot on the grill.

Colton stirred the coals and added more sticks. His eyes met hers. "You okay?"

"Yes. Just tired and a little sore."

"We should check your wound." He squatted beside her, and she allowed him to unwrap the bandage and apply more sanitizer. His hands were gentle. "The knee is badly bruised, but the swelling is down."

Belle watched Adam add water to the mice bucket and a daub of the peanut butter to the dowel before returning her gaze to Colton. “Thank you.”

He caressed her cheek. “You’re welcome.”

Light, fluffy snowflakes floated to the ground and Colton stood.

Belle shivered and huddled deeper into her coat. The snow frightened her. Texas got snow every now and again, but she knew the amount that would fall in these mountains would not be anything she was prepared for.

She looked into the darkening sky and whispered, “Please.”

Colton must have heard her whisper. “This snow won’t last, Belle. The worst storms will come in the next two or three months.”

“How do you know?”

His boyish grin lightened his expression. “Experience. I know hunters and sheepherders have been in these mountains. Many hunters will hunt in October during the regular rifle seasons, and they wouldn’t do this if winter snows made hunting too difficult.”

“Sheepherders? And you know this ... how?”

He bent and held out his hand. “Come. I’ll show you.”

She struggled to her feet, and he put an arm around her waist. “Lean on me. No need to aggravate your knee.”

He took her several hundred yards from camp and pointed at a name and date carved into an aspen trunk.

She touched the trunk. “Manuel Gonzalez. 1932. Wow, that’s a long time ago.”

"Herding sheep in this environment is a lonely job. I've seen many names and dates through the years."

"He wanted someone to know he existed." She paused. "I'd want people to know I existed if I had to stay in this overpowering, quiet world for several months with only sheep for company."

The snow fell faster, so they returned to camp.

Liam had opened one of the cans of green beans and heated them. He grimaced and handed Colton and her a plate. "Not much to eat tonight, but we have all the hot pine needle tea you want."

Adam indicated a large pan on the counter. "Hot water to wash with too."

They ate in silence in the shelter. Belle was tired of living from meal to meal, never knowing if she would even get to eat. She longed to sit in a comfortable booth in one of their restaurants eating whatever she desired.

I'd want these men dining with me. The thought startled her. In a short amount of time, they'd become a critical part of her life.

She envisioned introducing them to her parents and treating them to the best their restaurants offered. That wish gave her joy.

"When we get out of here, I want the three of you to come to Dallas for some exceptional food. My treat. You'll be able to eat all you want of whatever you want."

Adam grinned. "That sounds really good, Belle. I'll take you up on your offer."

Liam agreed.

Colton smiled. "Thank you. I'm sure I'd enjoy this, but if we get out of here any time soon, I have to return to

Montana. I have paid hunters coming through December. Maybe I could take a rain check?"

She stared at him. "After going through all this, you'd still return to the mountains to do almost the same thing you're doing now?"

"I have to, Belle. Outfitting brings in a large portion of my family's income for the year."

She chewed her bottom lip. "What exactly do you do when you outfit?"

"Hunters come to the ranch. We treat them royally. They sleep in comfortable beds and eat well before we ride out. Then my brothers and I pack them and their supplies to a base camp similar to this one. We set up tents and provide food for them to cook. In a week, we return and pack them, their supplies, and any game animals back to the ranch."

"Does this mean you're a guide? You find the game animals for the hunters?"

"No, my brothers have guide licenses. I just outfit."

Belle nodded and reached for her toothbrush and paste. She stood. "I'm tired. As soon as I take care of some things, I'm going to bed."

The men followed her to the basin of hot water with their toothbrushes.

Adam stacked the plates and utensils. "I'll be on KP."

Belle washed, then entered the shelter. Her knee ached, and her stomach growled. Tiredness hit her, so she lay down on the bed, pulled her coat up to her neck, and covered herself with the old mattress. She closed her eyes and listened to the night sounds and song of the forest.

Belle woke in the middle of the night to the splashes of mice falling into the bucket. She listened for quite a while, then turned on her side and caught the close scent of pine trees, cold, and mountains. *Colton?*

"We'll have meat tomorrow, Belle." She heard the smile in his whispered words.

"Uh-huh." She yawned and closed her eyes again.

CHAPTER 5

FOUR inches of snow covered the ground when Belle awoke. More continued to fall in this insulated, silent world, and she groaned. Snow in September.

Her bladder forced her out of the shelter, but she hurried back in. She spoke to no one in particular. "I'm going to sleep some more since we aren't going anywhere today."

The men must have agreed, because after they made quick trips out, built up the fire, and set water to boil, they returned to the shelter and pulled whatever covering they were using over themselves.

Belle shivered, and Colton whispered, "Turn your back to me."

She did.

He slid his arm under her coat and drew her against his length. He spread her coat over them. His heat warmed her, and she closed her eyes.

Somewhere on the edge of dreams, she thought she felt his kiss on her shoulder and heard him whisper, "Oh, Belle, how can we ever make us work?"

She mumbled something even she didn't understand.

Belle opened her eyes to the grumbling of her stomach. She faced Liam, her left arm over his middle. She watched his chest rise and fall and listened to his regular breathing.

Liam opened his eyes and smiled. "Hi, Belle. Was I snoring?"

"No." She removed her arm and sat up.

Adam and Colton were already outside. One of them had put the skillet on the grill to heat as they processed the mice.

Belle stretched. "I guess I'm cooking. Are you as hungry as I am, Liam?"

He nodded. "Starving. Wish we had more acorns."

Belle grimaced. "I wish we had prime rib, a hot buttered roll, or cherry pie."

She hobbled toward the opening, glad to see the snow had stopped and the sun had come out from hiding.

Liam stood. "Here, Belle. Hold on to me. I'll help you." He put his arm around her waist and snugged her to his right side. "Ready?"

"Yes."

They'd caught a couple of rats and a squirrel along with the mice, and all Belle thought about was how much more meat the larger rodents would add to the pot. She sighed. She wished for seasoning other than salt and pepper.

The more she thought of the seasoned meat, the louder her stomach rumbled.

She put a hand over her middle. "Be quite, beast."

Suddenly, an animal screamed somewhere in the distant forest.

Belle's eyes widened. "What is that?"

Colton listened. "A bull elk."

Another bull answered, this one closer to their camp. The animal made a grunting noise after his high-pitched scream.

Belle gazed toward the forest. "Why are they doing that?"

"They've started their rut. The sound identifies their location. Some of the cows are in heat, so the males want to keep their females away from other bulls. Some will fight for dominance and the right to breed the cows."

He grinned. "When my nephew, Landon, was a toddler, he sat on my brother Bill's lap and watched hunting videos for hours. When Bill took Landon into a sporting goods store with him, Landon noticed the elk mounts on the wall. He pointed and made a perfect young bull bugle—he could bugle before he could talk.

"A cow or young animal will sound like this." Colton made a series of high-pitched chirping sounds.

Belle stared, fascinated.

Liam put another stick in the fire. "Do you know any other wild animal sounds?"

Colton nodded. "A few." He made a gobbling sound. "This is a tom turkey." He clucked. "This is the hen. This is the sound turkeys make when they're fussing over food. When the toms fight, they're loud and noisy."

Adam dropped an armful of wood next to the fire pit. "What about bear?"

Colton shrugged. "Here's what a black bear sounds like when he's disturbed."

Belle hoped never to hear such a sound. She searched the forest around them as she fried the rodents and turned them to brown on the other side.

She stared at the outfitter's face. He seemed more human when he talked about what he knew than he had earlier, regardless of the passionate kiss. She didn't know what to do with his declaration, so she pushed his words to the back of her mind.

Liam turned to Colton. "Have you ever had bear encounters?"

He nodded. "A few nonviolent ones. When my brothers and I first started outfitting, we threw a rope over a tree branch and hung our ice chest high in the air. We didn't think any bear could get to the food inside.

"When we got back from hunting, the only thing we had left were handles attached to a frayed rope. The bear had climbed the tree, slid down the rope, and bounced on the ice chest until he broke the rope. We ended up with a cratered chest and no food.

"One other time, we left camp for the morning. When we came in for lunch, we saw tracks of a mother and her cub. They got into one of the hunter's hot and spicy pizza wraps and ate them. The spice must have been too hot for the bear. The mother punctured our water containers trying to soothe the burn."

He chuckled. "A cub sneaked into the tent while we were gone on another hunt. He put his muddy paws against the canvas. When he went inside, he must have gotten too close to the mouse traps we set before we left, because the traps were sprung. He tore his way through the corner of the tent trying to get out."

Liam laughed. "I can see his exit in my mind."

Belle's stomach complained. "Is bear meat good?"

Adam laughed. "Hungry, Belle?"

"Yes."

Colton shrugged. "Depends on what they've been eating. In my opinion, they're rank if they've had a steady diet of fish like the Alaskan bears. We make sausage out of the meat we get."

Sausage. Belle's stomach twinged. "Are bears dangerous?"

"They can be, especially if you get between a mother and her cubs, or if you run from them."

Liam poured a cup of hot pine needle tea. "If Belle and I are gathering acorns, what should we do if we see a bear?"

"Make noise. Most of the time, they'll leave. Whatever you do, don't run, and don't crouch down to hide. This excites them. You want to make yourself appear larger. Leave your backpack on if you are wearing one."

Belle shuddered. "Should we climb a tree?"

Colton shook his head. "Bears climb better than you do. Your hands and feet are no match for their teeth and claws. If you hear them make a popping sound with their jaws, like this," he demonstrated, "back up quickly. They're warning you to get out of their space."

Belle grimaced. "Where's the bear spray when we need a bottle?"

The rodents were ready, and Belle dipped out equal amounts onto each plate. Her eyes met Liam's. "When you pray, would you please ask God for more meat and something else to eat? I'm sure we would all appreciate this."

He grinned and nodded. "Will do."

Belle's portion disappeared faster than she wanted.

Colton stood and looked at the sky. "We have four hours before sundown." He glanced at Liam. "If you and Belle will search the area around camp for acorns or berries, Adam and I will search for any indication of the trail out."

He put on his coat and slung his rifle to his left shoulder. "Make sure you mark your direction like I showed you."

Liam nodded.

Colton's eyes met Belle's. He opened his mouth as if to say something, but no words came out. He turned and left, Adam at his heels.

Belle reached for her crutches and followed Liam. He carried one of the larger wash pans they'd found.

"No way I'm getting away from a bear using crutches." Belle's underarms hurt where the wood rubbed. "I'm going to have to get more padding on these."

She eyed the undergrowth. "Colton said to make noise. Maybe you should sing, Liam."

He grinned and tapped the bottom of the pan as if he played a drum or tambourine. The songs flowed without effort and the words sank into her soul. They brought her peace.

She didn't know how long they'd walked, but Liam's song came to an abrupt end.

Belle looked around. "What's wrong?"

He pointed. “Look. Chokecherries. Adam told me about these. You can eat them only when they turn dark after the first frost. The branches are loaded, Belle. Let’s see how many we can get.”

Liam studied the bushes and the ground around them. “Bears have been here.”

The hairs on the back of Belle’s neck rose.

Liam looked around. “How about you keep watch while I pick? I’ll hurry.”

She nodded. Could Liam feel her panic? Would a bear sense this? Belle took deep breaths and firmed her jaw. The men wouldn’t panic, so neither would she. “Okay.”

She moved to a spot where she could see more area but could keep Liam in her sight line. “Sing, Liam.”

He did. Gradually, her nerves calmed and she hummed along with him. The sense of forest and quiet seeped into her bones. She filled her lungs with the cool, clean air and listened to the bird calls and forest noises.

At first, the sound of something approaching didn’t trip her awareness, but the sudden stillness and lack of birdsong focused her attention. “Liam, something’s coming.”

He looked up.

Belle dropped a crutch and held the other in front of her, ready to strike if an animal came too close.

A sharp whistle sounded, and Belle relaxed. Colton and Adam warned of their approach.

Colton grinned when he caught sight of her. “You’re ready to fight, are you?”

“If need be.” Belle picked up the other crutch and put them under her arms. She tilted her head toward his left shoulder. "I think your rifle will do a better job, don't you?"

Adam pulled off his jacket to use as a container and started stripping the chokecherry branches of ripe fruit.

Colton popped a berry in his mouth. "Looks like Liam's prayers were answered. You'll have something different to eat tonight, though chokecherries have big seeds and not a lot of meat." He eyed her. "I found a stand of oak brush not too far from here. Will you help me gather the acorns? We don't have much time before we must return to camp."

"Yes." She followed him to the patch.

"You're getting easier on the crutches."

Belle nodded. "My knee doesn't hurt as much. Maybe I can get along without them soon."

Colton looked at the sky, then let down the rifle.

She pointed. "Why do you have a feather tied to the rifle barrel?"

"This shows me the wind direction."

Belle pulled at the hem of her red sweater and formed a basket. "Put the acorns in here."

He nodded and harvested faster than she ever had.

When her sweater bulged with acorns, he put more in his jacket. "Let's head back to camp. We don't want to be out here at dark."

A shiver slid up Belle's spine, and she peered into the forest as she followed him.

Adam and Liam had the fire going and a kettle of water warming when they walked in.

Belle dumped the acorns on the ground, and Adam and Liam went to work crushing the shells and separating the meat. The shelled acorns went into the kettle.

Colton put his haul on the ground and reached for a rock.

Belle eyed the berries as they all shelled acorns. “What happens if you eat the berries before they turn dark?”

Adam looked up. “They’re bitter and may make you choke. My throat swells. When the berries are ripe, my mom makes chokecherry jam.”

“Can we eat them now?”

The men thought this was a great idea.

Belle washed her hands and drank. Her eyes met and held Colton’s. “Did you find a way out?”

“Yes. Adam and I followed the trail for a mile. If the weather is good, we’ll head out tomorrow morning.”

Dread pulled at Belle. She hated the thought of leaving a place where humans had been—a place she felt safe—to face uncertainty. But what else could they do? They couldn’t stay here.

Without saying anything, Belle filled the other wash pan with water. She put the container on the grill with the acorns and waited for her wash water to heat.

When the water was hot enough, she started toward the shelter with the pan.

Colton stood. “Here, Belle. Let me carry that for you. You’re still limping.”

He set the container on the floor. “Once you’re finished, we’ll wash. I’ll start more water heating.”

Belle reached for the soap and cloth. If they would leave tomorrow, she intended to be clean when she started.

She made sure the men had their backs to her, then removed her clothing. She washed as quickly as she could, then put on the last clean garments she had. When her hand contacted the small bottle of perfume, she hesitated. Did she really need to use this?

Belle tossed her head. Feeling clean and smelling good gave her confidence, and she needed as much as she could get at the moment. She uncapped the lid and added a drop of the expensive scent behind each ear.

"I'm finished." She put on her coat and stepped out of the shelter. "I left the soap and cloth in the pan."

The men rose and took more hot water with them.

Belle poked at the fire with a long stick and stared at the flames until the men stepped out of the shelter. Only Liam wore his sweater. The other two were bare chested.

Adam held up his shirt and grimaced. "I'm going to have to wash this or burn the thing. The other shirt I had was damaged beyond repair when we crashed."

Colton put more water on to heat and tilted his head. "Same here. You can use the water first."

Adam dunked the shirt in the soapy water and scrubbed the underarms for several moments.

Belle smiled when he sniffed the shirt and returned the material to the water for more scrubbing.

Finally, the pilot rinsed his shirt in cold water, rang out the excess, and draped this on a stump next to the fire and sat.

Colton did the same thing, then poured himself a cup of hot pine needle tea and sat on the log next to Adam. She was glad they couldn't see her watching them in the dark.

She closed her eyes and listened to the pops and hisses of the fire and to the night sounds. The men talked in quiet tones, and the night air caressed her cheek. Sleep pulled at her, so she stood and stretched. "I'm going to bed. Goodnight."

Belle didn't know how long the men stayed up talking, but her half-dreaming self felt their warmth as they slipped in beside her.

They all smelled of pine needle tea and soap.

Belle slid deeper into her dream. The dream turned ugly, and screaming bull elk and bears figured prominently. She cried out, "A bear. Watch out, Liam!"

She tossed, turned, and muttered.

Liam's soft voice floated into her dreams. "I'm okay, Belle. You're having a nightmare."

Colton whispered near her other ear. "You're okay, sweetheart. You're safe. Liam is safe. Here, slide over and put your head on my shoulder. Get warm."

"Safe," she turned and slid over. The warmth of his embrace and his steadily beating heart comforted her. She sighed and moved closer to the heartbeat.

CHAPTER 6

THE feelings of warmth and safety were the first things Belle noticed when she surfaced from dreams into reality. The second was her sprawled position across Colton's chest. Her left cheek rested in the crook of his shoulder, and her right arm stretched across his middle. Both of his arms encircled her.

"Good morning." His soft, deep voice held warmth and amusement.

She startled awake. "Oh, my. I'm so sorry, Colton."

He grinned. "I'm not."

She rolled away from him and sat up. "We're leaving soon?"

He sat up too. Sunlight bathed the dark hairs on his chest with golden light. "Yes."

They moved outside, and Colton reached for his shirt. "Still damp, but this will have to do." He buttoned up and put on his coat.

Belle looked at the sunny sky. "No clouds, and the temperature feels warmer. The snow is almost gone."

They ate acorns and the remainder of the chokecherries. Belle glanced at the bucket trap. They wouldn't have any more rodents until they could set this at their next camp.

With the exception of the tarp, cordage, one water can, utensils for each, a wash pan, the quart pot, the mousetrap, a small jar of peanut butter, oil, and salt and pepper shakers, the men returned everything to the pit in their black plastic bags.

Liam wrote a thank you note using charcoal on a piece of bark and put this in the hole before the men covered the stash with the worn mattress and logs.

Adam emptied his backpack and replaced the contents with the folded tarp. Colton put Adam's things into his pack and slung the rifle to his shoulder. He watched Liam pack the utensils and supplies and attach the mouse bucket to the outside of the backpack.

Belle tied the aluminum wash pan to her pack. The outfitter had punched a hole in the lip and tied a piece of cord to this for easier traveling, and she could carry the pan even while using crutches. She thought she looked like someone with a sombrero on her back.

Liam asked for God's blessings before they stepped forward, and Belle's affection for him grew. He had a servant's heart and a kind, giving spirit, yet she sensed his underlying strength, as if he'd come through the fires of testing as a victor. He had a lot of assurance for someone his age.

His eyes met hers. "Why are you looking at me like that, Belle?"

"I wish I had a brother just like you. I've always wanted a sibling."

Liam smiled. "I'd like to have you for a sister."

Colton led, and Liam followed. She swung along behind him, and Adam brought up the rear. He chuckled and spoke in a low voice so only she could hear, “Neither Colton nor I want you for a sister, Belle.”

She glanced over her shoulder. “What?”

His eyes teased her. “You heard me.”

Belle pondered his words as they left camp. What did they want? What did she want? Adam and Colton made her feel safe. They were strong men with alluring qualities, but she had no confidence physical attraction alone would lead to anything but a shallow relationship and heartache.

They moved deeper into the shadowed forest, and Belle eyed the trees around her. She shivered. Did a bear watch them from behind an aspen or pine? Their footsteps made little sound in the wooded silence. If she couldn’t hear her own footsteps, how much chance did she have of hearing a soft-footed bear?

Belle didn’t know how long they walked, but the crutches now chafed her underams even with the extra padding she’d added. Her tension eased when they left the trees and stepped into a patch of meadow grass and sunshine.

Colton stopped and turned. “Belle, are you okay?”

“Yes.” Her answer lacked certainty.

Adam removed his heavy pack. “Let’s take a breather.”

Belle leaned against a boulder and uncapped her water bottle. She took several gulps.

Colton sipped from his bottle. “Best conserve your water. I don’t know where we’ll find the next source.”

They walked for another three hours—up and down slopes and around and over obstacles. Belle's energy waned. She got slower on the crutches and finally stopped, her head hanging.

Adam stepped up beside her and looked into her face. "Colton, we need to stop."

Colton turned, and his eyes widened. He lowered the rifle and his pack and strode toward her. He lifted her chin and studied her face.

Did she appear as haggard as she felt? She must look terrible if both men responded in such a manner. All Belle wanted to do was to curl up and sleep.

He nodded. "Let's make camp. Hang on, Belle. Liam will stay with you while Adam and I find a place for us. Drink more water. We have a few extra bottles with us."

The men left, and Belle dropped the crutches and slumped to the ground.

Liam sat and put his arm around her. "Lean against me and rest, Belle. You're eyes are sunken and your face is pale. I'll keep watch."

She drank, then leaned against his shoulder and closed her eyes. "Sing, Liam."

Liam squeezed her shoulder. "Belle, wake up. Adam and Colton are coming."

Belle forced her eyelids open and straightened.

Colton handed the crutches to Liam before he and Adam made a seat with their hands. "Put your arms around our necks, Belle. We'll carry you."

They moved much quicker than she could.

Belle looked around when they lowered her to her feet. She stared at the fire. A boulder about two feet high protruded from the ground. Over time, weather had eroded the rock until a large crack broke the stone in half. In this crack, the men had built a fire. Adam took the container from her and set this to heat across the crack.

They'd created a shelter nearby using a dead tree as the ridgepole. Many years ago, a pine sapling had fallen against another tree. Over time, the branches decayed and dropped leaving only the bleached and dried trunk. The intersection of the two trees formed a space barely large enough for the four of them. The men had draped the tarp over this and staked the bottom, then piled pine boughs on the inside and outside.

Colton poured water into one of the tin cups. "Drink, Belle. You're dehydrated. Adam and I need to see what we can forage for food. We'll be back by dark."

When they left, Belle drank more, then stood. "Maybe we can help by finding something to eat close by."

Liam nodded. "I hope we can find chokecherries or acorns. Drink more water before we leave, Belle."

"I'm not using the crutches. My underarms hurt."

They moved toward the trees. Liam marked their trail with the red strips they'd removed from the first camp.

Belle studied the plants as she meandered from one to another. She stopped at the edge of a rocky slope. "Look, Liam. Wild onions. We can season the rodents with these."

She pulled the metal fork she'd taken from the hunters' camp from her pocket and dug up several plants. She placed these in her sweater basket and imagined the smell of roasting meat and frying onions.

They also found more chokecherries and acorns. Belle ate as many of the berries as she harvested.

By the time Adam and Colton returned, she and Liam had shelled the acorns and put them on to leach.

Colton placed several bunches of different plants on the ground near the fire, and Adam dumped an armful of thick aspen sticks as long as his arm beside them.

Belle eyed the plants. "What did you find?"

Colton pointed. "Milkweed, lamb's-quarter, dandelion, and catnip."

"I found some wild onion."

Colton's eyes sharpened. "You didn't eat any of these, did you, Belle?"

"No. Why?"

He lifted one of the plants and pointed. "This is the poisonous death camas, not an onion."

Belle's heart raced. "How do you know?"

"By the lack of an onion or garlic smell and by the drier, grasslike stem. Look, the leaves of the death camas have a long, V-shaped indentation in them. The sides fold in easily. They don't smell like an onion even though they have a bulb-like one. I have to keep my cows out of places where this grows."

He held up a slightly different plant. "The onion has an oniony smell, and the leaf resembles a blade of grass with a slightly curved U-shape."

Colton threw half of her harvest away.

Belle tilted her head toward the stack of aspen branches. "We can eat those?"

Adam smiled. "Yes. We'll eat the inner bark."

As hungry as she was, Belle was game for anything edible.

Though Adam said they could eat the aspen bark raw, she boiled this with the milkweed. They washed and ate the dandelion and lamb's-quarter leaves raw, then sipped on the minty catnip tea.

Her stomach was satisfied for the moment. "Where are we going to get more water? We used most of what we had."

Colton stirred the fire. "I saw several elk tracks headed east. They are sure to lead to water eventually. I'll look tomorrow."

Belle leaned against a stump and unwound her bandage. The hole in her calf had scabbed, and the bruise on her kneecap had turned a mottled color. She rubbed the muscles above and at the side of the bruise, and the stiffness eased. If she could, she'd walk without the crutches when they left again.

She leaned forward, unzipped her backpack, and reached for the toothbrush, toothpaste, water bottle, and leggings.

Belle stood and walked behind a tree to brush her teeth and take care of business. She removed her pants and put on the leggings. She'd put the pants back on tomorrow.

When she returned, the men had brushed their teeth and used the remaining water in the pan to wash.

Colton banked the fire and touched part of the boulder closest to the tent. "Ah. Good. The rock is getting hot. This will throw heat into our shelter." He grimaced. “Sorry, Belle. Sleeping arrangements will be tight tonight.”

She sighed. “I can handle this as long as no one snores in my ear.”

Colton was right. The space was so tight, they could sleep only on their sides like nested spoons. The catnip tea mellowed Belle, and she closed her eyes. Warmth surrounded her, and her muscles relaxed.

Sometime in the night, Belle got too hot and started tossing. She pushed her coat away, and the night cold cooled her.

Belle didn’t open her eyes when she felt Adam and Liam get up and go outside.

Colton whispered in her ear. “Move over, sweetheart. You have more room.”

She scooted to the right, turned on her back. and put her right wrist on her forehead. Relief.

“Good morning, Belle.” Colton’s voice rumbled next to her face, and she opened her eyes. Again, her cheek rested on his shoulder, and her arm draped his middle.

She rolled to her back. “Where are the other two?”

He chuckled. “They got too hot and are sleeping outside next to the heated rocks.”

Belle slitted her eyes and looked outside. “The sun isn’t up yet.”

“No.”

She yawned and turned on her right side. “Then I’m going back to sleep. Wake me when breakfast is ready, okay?”

Colton moved closer and put his arm over her. “Will do. We’ll ask Liam to pray for an egg omelet with cheese.”

“Um. That sounds amazing.”

To watch bull elk battle ...

https://www.youtube.com/watch?v= FoqHoA2WeE.

CHAPTER 7

WHEN next she awoke, Belle was alone in the shelter and the men were outside talking, chewing on aspen bark, and sipping from cups of hot water.

She crawled out and pulled on her pants. Then she bent over her backpack and picked up her brush.

Belle took her time unsnarling her long hair. With each brush stroke, she wished for something rich and flavorful to eat.

The men stopped talking, and she looked up to see the three of them watching her. “Why are you all looking at me like that?”

Adam grinned. “You remind us of the beautiful things in life, Belle.”

Colton nodded and slung on his backpack and rifle. “We need to find water and the right trail. Will you be okay by yourself if Liam comes with us?”

Belle’s heart pounded behind her ribs. “I don’t know. Will I? You know better than I if I’m at risk.”

“If you don’t leave camp or eat anything we haven’t had before, you should be fine.”

“How long will you be gone?”

Colton looked at the sky. "Most of the day."

"What about bears?"

"They won't bother you, Belle. We don't have anything that smells good enough to lure them into camp."

She tightened her lips and put on her backpack. "No. I'm going with you. I don't want to stay here by myself. I know for certain my mind will start playing tricks on me if you all are gone for hours."

"What about your leg?"

"I don't have much pain. I'll use one of the crutches if I need to."

"All right. You have your water bottle?"

"Yes."

"Then grab some bark and acorns to chew on, and we'll go."

Adam and Liam headed southwest, and she and Colton moved toward the southeast.

She ate a handful of acorns. "Why are we always going south? Why not north or west?"

Colton continued walking, but spoke over his shoulder. "Many towns are built on the south, or warmer side of the mountains. To our west, the mountains are steep and cliffy. I didn't see much animal sign in that direction, which isn't good for us."

"Why?"

"This often means a lack of water or insufficient food in the area."

"What about the east?"

"I saw plenty of animal signs, but the trails often stayed up high."

"Is that bad?"

"We want to go downhill. To me, down means out eventually. Make sure you call out if you need to rest."

"Okay."

Belle tried to copy Colton's soft-footed movements. She watched her step and avoided sticks and rocks that might trip her.

They moved through trees and meadows. At the edge of the forest, Colton stopped and pointed. "Elk tracks."

Belle studied the prints.

He touched one of the impressions. "The big ones belong to the herd bull. The smaller are made by the cows and calves."

"You run cattle in the forest. How can you tell the difference between a moo cow track and an elk track?"

"Size and shape. The elk tracks are smaller and more oval than round. They also have a longer gait. Elk have curved toes with tips that taper. The two tips will point forward and toward each other. They have two dew claws on each foot. Look."

He traced the shape of the track. "Their front hooves are larger and wider than the back. Let's follow. They may lead us to water."

Belle didn't know how long they followed the tracks, but the elk led them deep into a shadowed quaking aspen grove. Her knee started to ache, and she opened her mouth to ask for a rest, when Colton stopped and held up his hand. He put his finger to his mouth and signaled her deeper into the trees.

They squatted behind some bushes and waited. For what, she didn't know.

Colton leaned close to her ear. “Smell.”

Belle inhaled. A musky, pungent odor curled her nose. “Ew.”

“We’ve found an elk wallow. Bull elk coat themselves in mud and their own urine.”

“Why do they do that?”

“They’re preparing for the rut. That odor you smell signals a bull’s rising testosterone levels. When they roll in mud and urine, they are walking advertisements for the cows. Stay here, and I’ll see if I can find the water source that feeds the wallow.”

She watched him ease around the muddy spot until he disappeared from view.

Bird song captured her attention, and she studied the trees around her. Several had skinned places on their trunks, and she wondered if these marks were made by humans or animals.

Filtered sunlight shone on her, and her muscles relaxed. She closed her eyes, but flies buzzed around her, interrupting her rest.

Colton startled her when he squatted beside her. She hadn’t heard or seen his approach. “Come on. We can fill our water bottles upstream.”

Belle stood and pointed to the trees. “What caused those marks?”

“The bulls use the trees as scratching posts to help them shed the velvet on their antlers.”

She followed him around the wallow and up a hill. He knelt beside a tiny seep of water and pulled out his water bottle. He hollowed out a spot near the source and let his bottle fill. “Give me yours.”

She handed him the metal container. "Is this water safe to drink?"

"Yes. I see no sign animals visit this spot, and the water is coming out of the hill, so the water isn't exposed to contaminants."

When her bottle was filled, Colton placed the other empty plastic bottles under the trickle.

Belle stood, put on her backpack, and reached for the crutch. "Will the trail take us out?"

"No. We need to head back. Maybe Liam and Adam found the way."

As soon as they reentered the trees, flies buzzed around her. She slapped at them. "They are so annoying."

"Here." Colton moved to a pine tree and stripped off several needles. "Rub the needles in your hands, and then wipe your hands on the hair around your face." He modeled for her.

"Ah. So, this is why you always smell like pine trees."

He grinned and nodded.

When they returned to camp, Liam and Adam waited for them.

Adam tilted his head. "We found the trail and a good spring a couple miles down. I thought maybe we could camp near the spring tonight."

The two had already packed the tarp in Liam's pack and moved his stuff into Adam's.

"Then let's go. Belle, do you need a rest?"

"Not right now. I'll let you know."

They packed everything in a matter of minutes and headed down the trail, this time, with Adam leading. Colton followed behind.

The downhill hike was harder on her knee than the uphill, so she used the crutch. She left the other behind. She was sure Adam slowed his normal pace for her sake.

Two miles seemed like ten.

When they got to the place they would camp, the men made short work of building a roomier shelter and starting a fire.

Adam rolled up a stump and told her to sit. "The spring is through those trees in a small arroyo. We'll fill the water can and all the bottles. This will take time because the flow isn't great."

By the time they returned with the first can of water, Belle had the wash pan ready. She'd ringed the fire with stones and put two larger, flatter rocks inside the ring to hold the pan above the flames.

Colton poured most of the water from the can into the tub and returned to the spring.

When they came back an hour later, Adam carried the can and Liam and Colton carried more plants and cut aspen limbs. Dinner. They hadn't had meat for two days, and Belle couldn't believe she wished for a plate of fried rodents.

After they finished what dinner they had, Belle looked at Liam. "Does God always answer your prayers? We asked for more food, but he doesn't seem to have answered this prayer."

He looked up from poking at coals. "He always answers them, but he doesn't always answer in the way I'd wish."

"Why?"

Colton and Adam listened.

Liam shrugged. "Sometimes, what I ask for isn't his will for me, so his answer is no. Sometimes, the answer is yes, but often, his answer is wait."

"Do you think his answer is no or wait to our request for more food?"

"I don't know, Belle. Sometimes, he wants us to trust him and not depend on our own strength."

"Will you ask him again?"

"Why don't you ask?"

"He'll listen to me?"

"In the book of Hebrews, chapter eleven, Scripture says that the one who comes to God must have faith, and that person 'must believe that he is, and *that* he is a rewarder of those that diligently seek him.' He hears the prayers of his children—those who come to him for forgiveness."

Belle processed his words. "Will you still ask?"

He smiled and immediately talked to God as if he were a loving father.

They baited the mouse bucket before they went to bed, and Belle listened and waited for the sound of splashing.

The night cold seeped in. She turned on her side, pulled her coat over her shoulder, and closed her eyes. Colton's arm came around her and drew her close. His warmth lulled her.

After a breakfast of fried rodents and edible plants, they started down the trail just as the sun topped the mountain peaks.

Belle glanced over her shoulder. Last night's shelter had been comfortable. She sighed. Maybe the next camp would be cramped like the previous one.

She marveled that her expectations had become so basic—food enough to fill her belly, all the clean water she could drink, shelter, and warmth.

Her life in Dallas seemed far away and dream-like in the harsh reality of the daily battle they fought with starvation.

She looked into the bright, late September sky. *Please. Will you provide more food?*

Before noon, they stopped to rest. Colton led them into the shade of an aspen grove and took off his rifle and pack.

Suddenly, the forest rang with elk screams, and the hairs on the back of Belle's neck raised. The noise sounded close by.

Colton handed his backpack to Liam and picked up the rifle. He didn't sling this over his shoulder, but carried the weapon in both hands.

He held up the rifle, and the feather on the end of his barrel moved in the breeze.

No one had to tell Belle to be quiet. Colton's posture instantly changed from cowboy outfitter to hunter. Adam's changed as well. They reminded her of large felines on the prowl.

Just before they left the woods and entered a meadow, Colton signaled them down.

A herd of tan and brown elk moved into this large clearing. They milled around and focused on two battling bulls.

Belle had never seen such a sight. The bulls went after each other with large, sharp antlers. They lowered their heads and pushed and butted. Their leg muscles strained against the other's weight.

She could smell the animals from where she sat. Other males in the area bugled, but Belle could not take her eyes from the battle.

Colton eased himself up beside a tree, raised his rifle to his shoulder, and fired.

The elk herd scattered—all except for a smaller bull who fell and lay still.

Colton made chirping sounds like one of the cow elk and waited a few minutes before walking toward the animal. He handed the rifle to Adam and pulled the knife and hatchet from their sheaths at his belt.

Belle didn't know if she wanted to watch what happened next, but this was dinner. God had provided.

She followed the others.

Colton pointed at part of an arrow sticking out of the bull. "An archer wounded him but didn't bring him down. He was swaying and looking sick. I doubt he would have lived much longer."

Belle stared at the downed elk. "How fresh is the injury?"

Colton's eyes met hers. "Probably early this morning."

Her eyes widened. "How do we contact this archer?"

"We probably won't. Archers can hunt off the beaten paths. They often backpack their meat out, so, if they don't use pack animals, they aren't limited to following a trail. I don't think there's much chance we'll ever catch up with this person."

His voice softened. “You may want to go sit under that tree until we’re finished. I don’t expect you’ll enjoy the sight of butchering.”

“This is dinner. I’ll watch.” She changed her mind as soon as they started.

“Belle,” Colton called, “we’re going to camp here so we can smoke some of the meat. We’ll need to preserve this to take with us.”

Adam and Liam bent several small aspen saplings toward each other. They tied the tops together to form an arch, then they interwove pine boughs to form a crude roof. Belle helped.

She hoped they wouldn’t get snow or rain. “Why didn’t you use the tarp?”

Adam pointed. “Colton is making a smoker.”

Belle followed them to the other side of the meadow. The outfitter had made a tripod as tall as his head. Between the legs, he’d tied up drying racks of small, interwoven branches. He’d used fibers he’d taken from the pine tree root ball near the crash site to tie them together and to the frame.

Adam started a fire between the tripod legs while Colton laid strips of elk meat across the racks. They draped and tied the tarp around the tripod and left an opening at the top and bottom.

When the fire burned down, Adam added fresh pine and aspen boughs. These created thick smoke.

Colton looked up. “Liam, will you start another fire close by? We’ll cook some of the meat now.”

Liam did, and Belle brought a couple of armloads of wood.

Her stomach growled continually at the thought she would soon have all the red meat she could eat. She pulled the oil, salt, and pepper from her bag and waited for the pan to heat.

Adam dropped the first chunks in the hot, oiled pan, and Belle's mouth watered at the aroma. She seasoned the elk and tried not to take a bite of the still raw meat.

She heaped the men's plates and continued to cook what they brought her.

Colton came to the fire, dried blood on his hands. He unscrewed one of the water bottles and handed this to Belle. He cupped his palms as she poured the liquid over them. The outfitter scrubbed off the blood, then dried on his pants legs. "We need to stay here a day or two to eat and to smoke as much meat as we can. We'll need to look for another water source first thing in the morning."

They waited for Liam to pray. When he said amen, Belle picked up the first piece of meat with her fingers. She looked at the texture and color, then took a bite. She closed her eyes as she chewed. "This is the best meal I've ever eaten."

The men laughed.

Colton watched her as he ate. "Don't get in a hurry. Your stomach won't take a lot of heavy meat all at once. Nice and easy."

Belle savored every bite. When she'd satisfied the demands for food, she sipped at more of the catnip tea.

Stars appeared, and she stood. "I'm headed to bed."

Adam stood too. He held out his hand for Colton's rifle. "I'll take first watch."

Colton nodded and handed him the weapon. “Wake me when you want me to spell you.”

“I will.”

Liam finished his plate of food. “I can take a turn too. I’ve used a rifle before.”

Both men nodded.

Belle watched Adam leave. “Why is he watching?”

Colton’s eyes followed the pilot. “Bears and other night animals will be able to smell the meat. Adam will keep the fires going and will run off any hoping to get a taste of our food.”

A shiver traced up Belle’s spine as she reached for her toothbrush, paste, and water bottle. “Will we be safe enough in the shelter? We don’t have any walls.”

Colton nodded. “We’ll build a fire and rock shield to bounce the heat back into the shelter. Animals will be more interested in the food than in us.”

Belle lay on her back for a long time and listened to Liam’s rhythmic breathing and for any whisper of sound indicating an animal approached. She couldn’t relax.

Colton turned to face her. He whispered, “Don’t worry, Belle. You’re safe. Get some sleep. Here, move closer.”

She rested her head on his shoulder and put her arm across his waist. “This is becoming a habit, Colton.”

He chuckled and drew her closer. “A good one.”

Belle woke for a moment each time the watch changed, but she didn’t come fully alert until the first rays of sun touched her eyelids.

Warmth surrounded her, and she opened her eyes. Colton slept on her right and Adam on her left.

She looked toward the smoker and watched Liam feed the fires. She grinned at the thought of more food.

Adam moved, and her eyes met his.

He caressed her cheek. “Hello, beautiful. Why are you smiling like that?”

Colton’s eyes opened. They didn’t look friendly when he saw Adam’s palm on her cheek.

Belle sat up and stretched. “We get to eat today, that’s why.”

Adam chuckled and stood. He put on his shoes. “That is worth getting up for. I’ll see how Liam is doing.”

Colton reached for his boots. “Do you like the pilot?”

Belle turned to him. He kept his back toward her as he put them on.

“I like him a lot, but if you’re asking if I’m interested in Adam in a romantic way, then I’d say no. I should be. He’s strong, handsome, has a good job, and is one of my protectors, but, surprisingly, one of the other protectors holds my affections.” She paused. “Liam is quite a catch, don’t you think?”

Colton spun around and studied her face, shock lurking in his eyes. Belle smiled when he realized she teased him.

He exhaled. “You had me worried for a moment.”

She grinned. “I did, didn’t I?”

He nodded, his eyes glittering. “I’m the man who holds your affections?”

Belle stood and held out her hand. “Since you’re the only remaining protector, love, I’d say that is a good guess. Now let’s eat.”

CHAPTER 8

THEY ate several times throughout the day, but Belle didn't think she'd ever feel full.

Adam took Colton's rifle and came back with a couple of birds he called ruffed grouse. Within ten minutes the birds were plucked, gutted, and frying.

Colton took the rifle. "I didn't hear you shoot."

Adam smiled. "I didn't. I killed the first grouse with a thrown rock and the second with a long stick. I got lucky."

Belle seasoned the meat and looked into the sky. *Thank you.* She knew Adam's success had nothing to do with luck.

She turned the meat and added wild onions. Now that she knew the difference between death camas and the onions, she looked for them wherever they walked. She also kept an eye out for sweet oxeye daisies and wild violet. She was glad Colton had shown her these plants. They were her favorites.

They all now foraged wherever they stopped.

Belle watched Colton cut more strips from the carcass. Occasionally, he'd throw small pieces of meat to a couple of white and gray-blue birds he called camp robber jays. The curious birds were fearless.

One hopped on Colton's hand and took the meat from his palm. Before long, several more of the birds stood around eyeing the meat and the outfitter.

He looked up and caught her watching him, and his eyes lit. After her admission this morning, she often felt the warmth of his gaze. He also smiled more than he used to.

Colton removed the drying racks from the smoker and added more racks of meat then walked to her and offered her a piece. "See what you think."

She took a bite. "Delicious. More, please."

He handed her another and put a strip in his own mouth.

"Are we leaving tomorrow?"

Colton looked into the sky. "Yes. We need to get off the mountain. We've been here ten days already, and I can feel a change in the weather."

Their loads were heavier than usual when they started out at daylight the next morning, but no one wanted to leave any food or the tarp behind.

They returned to their previous camp and filled all the water bottles before starting down the trail.

Belle looked over her shoulder before following the men.

A sense of urgency made her glance at the heavy, dark clouds. They continued to build, and the breeze touching her skin chilled.

They walked for hours. A couple of times, they lost the way and had to backtrack until they found more markings. The extra walking exhausted her.

In the middle of the day, they rested on the trail and ate and drank.

Colton sat beside her. “How are you holding up?”

“I’m okay, but I don’t know how much energy I have left.”

“We’ll camp in a couple of hours. We’re dropping in elevation. Did you notice the change in vegetation?”

“No, I’m too tired to notice much.”

“Shall I carry your pack?”

“No, love. Yours is heavy enough without me adding to your load. I’ll do my part.”

Adam and Liam looked from her to Colton. One corner of Adam’s mouth curled, and he nodded. “I could see this coming days ago.”

“What?” She put a piece of the smoked meat in her mouth and chewed.

“Since when is the outfitter your love, Belle?”

She smiled. “I guess he’s grown on me since we crashed.”

Colton laughed. “I’ve known from day one, but Belle took a little longer to realize this. We’re as unlikely a pair as a person can think of, aren’t we?”

Liam grinned but said nothing.

Lazy snowflakes ended their meal, and they picked up their packs and continued. Within an hour, the snow started sticking. They picked up their pace. After three more hours, Belle stumbled. “Can we rest for a few minutes?”

Colton reached for her. "Hang on, sweetheart."

Adam stopped under a ponderosa pine. "Colton, the trail is getting slippery. We need to camp here."

Belle looked around. "Here? As in the middle of the trail here?"

The pilot nodded. "Yes. We don't want to chance ending in one of those steep canyons because we took the wrong path."

Colton took out his knife and handed this to Liam. He gave the hatchet to Adam. They cut several pine boughs and laid a thick mat of them in the middle of the trail. Liam brought firewood.

Colton took the magnesium striker out of his pack and the cotton balls Belle had given him from her cosmetics bag and struck sparks into the dry mass. Soon they had a fire.

They ate and then laid on the boughs and pulled the tarp over them. The four of them huddled together, and Belle prayed they wouldn't be buried under a foot of snow when they woke the next morning.

Colton pulled her close and kissed her neck. "Sleep now, sweetheart. You're going to need all your energy tomorrow."

She turned to face him. "Will we get out of here alive?"

He stroked her hair. "I hope so, but I don't know our future. Liam, Adam, and I will do our best, Belle. We have a lot to live for, don't we?"

Adam spoke from the other side of Liam. "Do you know what the hardest part of all of this has been for me? Losing a crew member and passengers on my watch."

Liam lifted the tarp and looked at him. "Would you have done anything differently? Did you make any mistakes?"

Adam remained silent for several moments. "I did everything the way I'd been taught. I would not have done anything differently."

"Then why do you take responsibility for their deaths? You aren't the one who decides who lives or dies, my friend."

He grimaced. "Why did they die and we live, Liam?"

"Do you want to hear what the Bible says?"

"Yes."

Liam quoted, "'It is appointed unto men once to die, but after this the judgment.' Ready or not, all of us will meet God when he calls. But God also says for those who have accepted Jesus Christ as their Savior, they are passed from death to life, and no condemnation rests on them."

Adam waited ten heartbeats. "Were you allowed to live because of us?"

Liam chuckled. "Probably. God calls you all to him. I'm just his messenger. I've been bought with the price of the blood of Jesus Christ. Sometimes, I need reminding that he is still in control. The crash certainly did this."

No one said anything, and as the temperature dropped, they huddled together and faded into sleep.

They traveled for four more days, sleeping in the open in the evenings.

Colton said the hunters would not take four days to get to camp.

Belle chewed her lip. "But we've already been walking for days. Surely we're closer."

He nodded. "We don't know where we're going, and we have to do a lot of backtracking. We are closer, sweetheart, but I can't tell you by how much. Different groups of hunters followed game trails and cut their own. This high up, they all used pack animals who walk faster than we do."

Each day brought new challenges. The trail disappeared, and they had to stop several times until Adam and Colton found the way out. When they didn't like what they saw, Liam reminded them God knew where they were and prayed for direction.

Belle marveled. After he talked to God, they always found a clue.

Yesterday, they'd had to cross what Colton called a snowfield. Avalanches from the winter before had piled several feet of snow into a deep, dark crevice. The snow had not melted totally, and ugly holes pockmarked the steep slide and showed the creek twelve feet below.

Belle's eyes widened and her heart raced. "Surely, we're not crossing this."

Colton nodded and pointed. "Elk have crossed here regularly. See the trail on the other side?"

The thin eyebrow of the path continued far down on the other side of the gully.

Belle wiped at the sweat now beading her forehead and eyed jagged rocks protruding from one of the melted spots nearby. "What if I fall and start sliding?"

Colton traced the way they would go with his eyes. "You won't, but if you do, spread your arms and legs."

Belle had no trouble envisioning her spinning slide down the mountain and her sudden death as she fell into one of the pits and onto the jagged rocks beneath.

Adam touched her shoulder. "Breathe, Belle. You're hyperventilating again."

She sat, bent her knees, and put her face between them. She sucked in as much thin air as she could and tried not to think of crossing the slide.

Colton sat beside her. "We'll rest here for a bit. Good girl. Take more deep breaths and unclench your fists."

Belle looked up.

Adam handed them all strips of elk jerky and pulled out his water bottle.

Liam sang a happy song, and Belle's muscles relaxed.

Thirty minutes later, Colton stood and slung on his backpack and rifle and offered her his hand. "Come on. You can do this. You want to get off the mountain, don't you?"

Belle tightened her lips and firmed her jaw. "Yes. Let's go."

Trudging through a foot of snow took every bit of Belle's energy and attention. She'd already fallen several times. When Colton helped her up, she caught an expression of desperation in his eyes.

"Drink more water, Belle."

"We don't have much."

"We can melt snow. You're getting dehydrated, and you can't afford to in this weather."

She drank and chewed on smoked meat. Last night, she'd dreamed they had walked and walked and gotten nowhere.

As they moved lower in elevation, the snow abated and they could see the ground through the patches.

Adam stopped and raised a hand. Colton moved forward, and the two stared at a fork in the trail. They talked about splitting up to see where each led.

"No. We're to wait here." Liam's voice was firm and sure.

Both men looked at him, uncertainty clear in their stances.

"Wait." Liam insisted.

Adam shrugged. "Okay. We might as well start a fire and have something to eat."

They ate and glanced often at Liam.

Suddenly, Colton straightened and stared down the left-hand trail. "Riders are coming. I hear the jingle of their spurs and the creak of saddle leather."

They stood and waited.

A man and woman dressed in camouflage clothing and fluorescent orange vests rode up to them leading three pack animals. Surprise widened their eyes. The man stared. "Are you the plane crash survivors? We saw your pictures on the news before we came here to hunt."

Adam nodded and introduced himself and the rest of them. "Will you help us get out of here?"

The woman dismounted. "Sure. I'm Gloria Easton. My husband is Jack. You look like you're all in. Good thing you got out when you did. The weather people predicted three feet of snow in the high country tonight."

Colton swung onto the saddle of the largest mule and reached down for Belle. He pulled her into the saddle in front of him and wrapped his arms around her.

Jack nodded. "Looks like you know what you're doing." He unsnapped the mule's lead from the one in front of him and handed up the rope.

Belle watched Adam and Liam mount before they started down the trail.

"Thank God for Liam," Colton whispered near her ear. "We could have wasted hours on the wrong trail."

They rode and rode, and Belle slumped against Colton's chest.

His arms tightened around her. "I've got you, sweetheart. Close your eyes and rest now."

She didn't open them until the mules stopped at a horse trailer.

Gloria shook her head and tsked. "Poor thing. Get her in the truck, Mr. Morgan. We'll turn on the heater. There's a blanket in the back seat. Put that around her."

Belle leaned against Colton's shoulder, but her head kept falling forward when she dozed.

"Come here, Belle." He tugged her onto his lap and she rested her cheek against his heart.

The strong beat comforted her and gave her hope. They would be okay. She would be okay. *Thank you.*

CHAPTER 9

BELLE couldn't rest. Though exhaustion permeated her muscles, the muted sounds of soft-footed nurses, the purring of the heater, the beeps of monitors, ringing telephones, and the low-voiced conversations of staff and visitors rang in her ears.

One of the nurses came in to check her vitals.

"Where are my friends?" Belle's words sounded like a dry croak.

The nurse smiled. "Mr. Sutherland and Mr. Swanson share a room across the hall, and Mr. Morgan is next door."

When she left, Belle eased out of bed, took hold of her I.V. stand, and rolled to the door. She peeked out. No one looked in her direction, so she slipped into Colton's room and stood at the side of his bed.

He opened his eyes and smiled. "Hi, you."

"I can't rest. This place is much noisier than the mountains. People are always coming and going. May I—?" She pointed.

Colton moved to one side of the bed and lifted the covers.

She slid in, rested her cheek on his right shoulder, and stretched her arm across his chest. He held her. She sighed and closed her eyes.

"Wake up, Belle. We have company."

She mumbled.

He kissed the top of her head. "Use English, sweetheart. Our visitors don't speak French."

Belle forced her eyes open. A couple in their sixties and a man who looked like a younger version of Colton stood beside the bed.

The older man frowned. "You're flat on your back and asleep in the middle of the day. Does this mean you're more dead than alive, Son?"

Colton grimaced. "Hey, Dad. I'm fine considering I survived a crash and fourteen unplanned days in the Rockies."

The younger man grinned. "I've never seen my brother snuggling with any woman, Dad, much less a gorgeous blonde. He must be better than okay."

Belle struggled to sit up, but Colton kept his arm around her. "Wait, I'll raise the bed."

She sat up and blinked the sleep out of her eyes.

"Oh, honey, you've had a rough time, haven't you?" Colton's mother came around to her side and put her hand on Belle's arm. "Stay still until you know you can stand without getting light-headed. Here, let me get you a drink of water."

She poured water into Colton's plastic cup and handed this to Belle.

Belle drained the cup. "Thank you."

She nodded. "You're welcome."

Colton sat up too. "Mom, Dad, Brian, this is Belle St. John. Belle, these are my parents, Henry and Janet Morgan, and my younger brother, Brian."

Belle attempted a smile. "I've heard a lot about you and your ranch. I'm pleased to meet you. Sorry I'm not in much of a condition to greet visitors."

"Never mind that, honey. We're pleased to meet you, and we're glad you got out of the mountains alive."

"Belle?"

They all looked toward the door.

Belle eased off the bed and stood. "Mom? Dad?" Tears leaked from the corners of her eyes.

Her parents rushed into the room and embraced her. Both wept openly.

Dad hugged her again. "We're so glad you're alive, baby girl. The Civil Air Patrol and Search and Rescue were about to call off the search until an observer spotted your plane. They knew someone survived because they saw the arrow made from suitcases. They called us and asked for something of yours they could use to give the bloodhounds your scent. We flew out as soon as we heard."

Mom touched her face. "You've got dark circles under your eyes, and you've lost a lot of weight. Are you okay, darling?"

"I am, but I wouldn't be if Colton, Adam, and Liam hadn't made sure I lived."

She turned and waved toward the others. "Mom, Dad, this is Colton Morgan, his parents Henry and Janet, and his brother, Brian. These are my parents, Jackson and Holly St. John." She hugged them again. "I'm so glad to see you."

Dad stepped closer to the bed and offered his hand to Colton. "Thank you for saving my girl."

Colton shook his hand. "My pleasure, sir. She's worth saving."

"Let's get you back to your room, darling." Mother put her arm around Belle's waist, and Dad reached for her I.V. stand.

Belle's eyes met Colton's. "See you later."

He nodded, and Belle shuffled to her room. She got back in bed and her mom tucked her in.

"Belle," Mom hesitated, "you were in Colton's bed."

Belle blinked. Her tired brain tried to focus. "Yes. I've been in his bed from the time we crashed. I was not dressed for mountain survival and was always cold, especially after I hurt my knee and Adam had to remove the lower part of my pants leg. I always got the middle spot.

"At the first shelter, Adam slept on my right and Liam on my left. In the next shelters, Liam slept on my right and Colton on my left. They were as warm as radiant heaters. In case you're wondering, nothing inappropriate happened there or here."

Dad frowned. "If you were cold, you could have asked the nurse for a blanket."

"I wasn't cold, Dad, just restless and uneasy. I'd gotten used to hearing Colton's heartbeat and smelling his scent. To me, he represents strength and safety."

Mom stroked her forehead. "Uneasy about what?"

Belle shrugged. “About a lot of things.”

Dad picked up her hand. “Do you love him? He seems wild to me, though that isn’t the exact word I want.”

Belle’s eyelids drooped. “I love them all. They are my family. They protected and cared for me.”

“But Colton?”

Her eyes closed. “Wild or not, he’s the man who has my heart. I can’t imagine life without him.”

Dad kissed her cheek. “We’ll come back later. Get some sleep.”

Mom patted her hand. “I brought you some clothes when you’re ready for them.”

“Thanks. I love you both so much.”

Belle awoke feeling more like herself. She didn’t know how long she’d slept, but all she wanted now was to soak in a bathtub surrounded by thick, scented bubbles. She decided a hot shower and clean hair would feel just as good.

Nurse Linda came in with a tray of food.

Belle smiled and sat up. “I don’t know why hospital food gets such a bad rap, but I’ll take this any day over what I’ve had to eat for the last two weeks.”

She laughed and set the tray on the rolling table. “I can imagine. What *did* you eat?”

“Whatever food we found in our bags, then acorns, chokecherries, edible plants, mice, squirrel, grouse, and elk.”

Linda stared. “You ate mice?”

“Yes.”

Linda filled up Belle's water pitcher. "The press are here, so prepare yourself. The aviation investigators are interviewing the pilot at this very moment. They'll want to question you too, though personally, I think they could wait a few more days."

Belle sighed. "Can you keep them away from me for a while? At least until I've showered and had more food?"

"I'll try. Do you need help? The doctor will be here in an hour with your parents."

"I think I can manage." Belle looked around the room. "Who are all the flowers from? The place looks and smells like a florist shop."

Linda read the notes attached to each.

Friends, family, co-workers, and suppliers.

Belle pushed the table away and shifted to the edge of the bed.

"Slow and easy." Linda moved to Belle's side and waited for her to stand. "I'll start the water for you. Your mom left your shampoo, conditioner, and body wash on the sink. Your blow dryer, brush, and curling iron are in the cabinet."

"Great. Could I get an extra bowl of the apple crumble? I'm still hungry."

Linda laughed. "Of course. Anything else?"

"Maybe two of them?"

"Sure."

By the time the doctor and her parents showed up, Belle had dressed in a silk blouse, cashmere sweater, and warm slacks. She'd dried and styled her hair and waited in the chair by the bed for her visitors. She listened to the quietness.

Doctor Anderson smiled. "You look much better, Miss St. John."

"Thank you. I feel much better."

"The good news is your knee X-rays showed nothing broken or cracked."

Dad sighed his relief. "What about her blood work? Is my daughter okay?"

He nodded and looked at her. "Your blood work shows you're healthy despite being undernourished."

Belle tilted her head toward the two empty plates. "I'm working on that. When can I leave?"

"The other men in your group asked me the same thing. I'd say if you feel well, you can leave in a couple of days."

The doctor left. As soon as he did, Liam and Adam showed up. She stared. With their beards removed and their hair and clothes clean, they looked like different men.

She smiled and signaled them into the room. "Adam. Liam. Meet my parents." She introduced them.

Dad pumped each of their hands. "Belle has told us how instrumental you were in saving her life. My wife and I are eternally grateful."

She moved to the bed so they could sit on the couch and in the recliner. Belle smiled. "You both clean up well."

Liam grinned. "You do too, Belle. Much better than we do."

Dad studied the two. "If you are in the Dallas area, please be our guests. We will house and feed you and show you a royal time."

They both nodded.

Mom turned to Adam. “Will you return to flying, Captain Sutherland?”

“Call me Adam, Mrs. St. John. Yes, I’m going to take time off to see my family, but I’ll be flying again.”

“Where is your home?”

“In the Denver area.”

Belle studied his face. “Did you give the investigators the pictures? Did you give them the bag?”

“Yes. I gave them the GPS coordinates of the crash site too, so teams are on their way up now.”

Liam chuckled. “Seems like we’re going to be famous, Belle. A movie producer is here wanting information for a possible documentary, and an author offered to ghostwrite our stories.”

“What did you tell them?”

Adam frowned. “We didn’t agree to anything. Our situation in the mountains is still raw for me. I need more time to process.”

Dad nodded. “That is wise. If you want, I can act as your representative. You can send them to me if they have questions.”

Colton entered. “I thought I heard your voices.”

Belle blinked. She’d never seen the outfitter without facial hair.

He grinned. “What? You’re staring at me like I left shaving cream on my face.”

She patted the bed beside her, and he sat close.

He leaned in and whispered. “You’re stunning.”

She clasped his hand and returned the whisper. “You are too.”

Colton chuckled. "I'm glad you think so."

Adam tilted his head. "Mr. St. John has agreed to field questions from those reporters, writers, and movie people on our behalf if you want him to."

Colton grimaced. "Great. I don't want to talk to any of them."

Liam teased, "You don't want to be famous?"

"Absolutely not. I have enough to deal with."

Dad rubbed his chin. "If you want them to leave you alone, you might consider making a joint statement soon and then setting a date you'll talk more in-depth with them."

Mom nodded. "But the crash investigators must interview you, Belle. They told me to ask you to meet with them tomorrow morning."

She sighed. "Adam, what will they ask me?"

"They'll want your description of what you saw and heard before, during, and after the crash. They'll ask several questions that might seem irrelevant to you, but answer them the best you can."

"Excuse me."

They all turned toward the door.

Colton smiled. "Mom?"

"Your dad and I ordered food for all of us. The food is here. The staff has been understanding about our wish to eat in private, away from the curious crowds, so they've provided a meeting room for us."

Janet Morgan smiled at Liam and Adam. "Your folks just showed up, so they're waiting for you."

Dad stepped to the door and lowered his voice. "I'd like to help defray the cost, Mrs. Morgan."

"No need, Mr. St. John. The restaurant manager heard about the rescue, and he gave us a drastically discounted rate. He sends his best wishes."

Colton stood and reached for Belle's hand. "Come on, I'm starving."

Belle grinned. "I know what you mean."

The happiness in that room filled Belle with joy. Because Liam and Adam felt like family, their relatives did too. They embraced, cried, hugged, and talked all at once. Belle imagined this is what Christmas might sound and look like at the Morgan's place.

Colton whispered near her ear. "We need to talk soon, Belle."

She nodded. "Come to my room after our families leave for the night and the nurses have checked our vitals."

Colton tapped on her door, and Belle marked her place in the Gideon Bible and looked up.

He eased into the room and closed the door. He stared at her, hands on his jean-clad hips and feet spread. "I love you, Belle. With everything that's in me, I love you."

She stood and walked to him. "I love you too."

He tugged her into his embrace and kissed her. "So where do we go from here?"

She caressed his smooth cheek. "Where do you want us to go?"

His voice roughened and his arms tightened. "I want to marry you. I want us to have children together. I want to teach them the joys of ranch life and family. I want us to grow old together, but how can I ask this of you, when you have a far different life? I could never live in a city, Belle. I would die inside."

Belle considered for several moments. "The mountain changed me, Colton. The quietness seeped into me as well as the smell of pines and clean air. I'm not sure I can get used to the noise and busyness again."

His green eyes glittered. "Does this mean you'll marry me?"

She chewed her bottom lip. "You don't know how much I want to say yes, but what if I can't overcome my big city ways? What if I can't survive in your environment? Our marriage would disintegrate."

He pushed a strand of hair behind her ear. "You lived through our experience, Belle, so I know you can survive in Montana. I wouldn't ask you to go to the mountains with me unless you wanted to."

She smiled and toyed with a lock of his hair. "I liked being in the mountains with you, my protector and hero."

He kissed her until the breath left her lungs.

Reluctantly, he pulled away. "Come to my home for Christmas, Belle. Bring your parents. See what you think, then I'll ask you again, okay?"

"Okay. Did you lose business while you were off the grid?"

"No, my brothers took care of things, but I have to get back. We have archers coming for the last part of this season. Then the general hunts for deer and elk start the last of October and run through Thanksgiving. Our muzzleloader season starts the first week of December and goes to the middle of the month. I'll be finished by the time you and your folks come."

"Then if this is going to be our last night together for a while, stay for a bit. We can watch television."

Belle raised the head of the bed and moved over. She flipped on the television and turned the volume to low.

Colton stretched out beside her and pulled her close. His nostrils flared, and he inhaled. "Did I tell you yet how good you smell? You make me glad I'm alive."

CHAPTER 10

REPORTERS and television crews learned of their release and waited in the lobby. Belle cringed. She did not want to face them yet.

Dad patted her arm. “Don’t worry, hon. You and your mom will take the stairs. Wait for me in the car until I speak with the press. Better say your goodbyes now.”

Liam stepped forward and opened his arms. “Bye, Belle. Make sure you keep in touch. You have my number. Call any time you need to talk.”

She went into his arms. He kissed her forehead, then rested his against hers. “God has your back, Belle. Trust him.”

“I will, Liam. Take care of yourself. I love you.” She kissed his cheek.

“I love you too.” He stepped away, and Adam took his place.

The pilot wrapped her in a hug, then kissed her forehead, cheek, and lips. “Goodbye, Belle. I’ll see you in a month. I’m accepting your parents’ invitation, so don’t be surprised when I show up.”

She brushed away a tear. “I’ll look forward to seeing you again.”

He grinned. “You know, I thought about giving Colton a run for his money where you were concerned, but I couldn’t compete with the intensity of the feelings you had for each other from the start.”

“I love you, Adam. You’re part of my family now.”

“I love you too, Belle. Take care of that ornery outfitter who is giving me the evil eye for kissing you.”

She glanced at Colton. “Seems to me he can take care of himself.”

Adam laughed and slung his backpack over his shoulder. “Yes, I guess he can.”

Colton stepped forward and touched her face. “Call me often, I need to hear your voice. Even if I’m packing and don’t have cell service, leave a message.” He drew her close. “Staying apart from you for almost three months will be pure torture.”

“I will. You call when you can.” She wrapped her arms around his neck and lifted her mouth for his kiss.

After several moments, Dad cleared his throat. “Time to go, Belle.”

She and Colton parted slowly.

Colton took a deep breath and followed her dad and the others to the elevator. He looked back at her.

“Are you ready, darling?” Mom pointed toward the stairs. “We need to be inside the car before the reporters realize you’re not with the men. Dad already loaded your bag.”

“I’m ready, Mom.”

Belle slid into the back seat beside her mother.

Dad came out ten minutes later. “Let’s go home.”

Belle sighed and curled her bare feet under her as she relaxed on the luxurious couch in the penthouse.

Dad handed her a bottle of water and sat down next to her. "Turn on the news. I think we made the top story tonight."

Not long into the program, Dad appeared. He thanked the hunters who brought the survivors out of the mountains, the hospital staff who cared for them, and the restaurant owner who provided a meal for them and their families.

"They will be leaving the hospital in a moment, but they are still trying to process this terrible experience. Please be sensitive to their needs and refrain from questions until a later time. They have agreed to speak with you soon, so please be patient."

Adam and his parents exited first, and the cameras zoomed in on his handsome face. The reporters couldn't restrain themselves. "Captain Sutherland! Captain Sutherland!"

They threw questions at him, but Adam smiled and lifted a hand. "We'll talk later." He got into the limo Dad had requested to take them to the airport.

Liam and his folks followed. His parents looked wide-eyed at the cameras and gave nervous smiles before entering the same car.

Belle's heart beat faster when the Morgans stepped outside. Brian loved the attention, but anyone within a hundred yards of Colton could see how much he hated the cameras and the questions. He walked past the reporters as if they weren't there and ducked inside the limo.

Dad chuckled. "His response is going to make them more determined to question him."

Belle smiled. "They'd have to catch him first. I don't know of any one of them who could keep up with Colton in the woods. He'd put on camo and disappear before they knew what happened."

The woman reporter continued. "And where is the elusive heiress, Arabella St. John, who, in addition to Captain Adam Sutherland, Liam Swanson, and Colton Morgan also survived the crash?"

Belle jerked upright. They flashed a picture of her taken last year at a charity event. "Her father says she is unable to talk right now, but will be available at a later date. Let us hope this will be soon."

"I hate being cheap entertainment for these people, Dad."

"I know, baby girl, but you're a miracle, and people want to know miracles still exist."

"Do you think the reporters will follow the limo to the airport and harass them there?"

Dad chuckled. "Probably, but the limo didn't go to the airport, at least not with your friends inside. The pilot's family drove down from Denver, so the driver dropped them off at a nearby parking garage. I'm sure they left immediately.

"The Morgans got out in the parking garage and took the taxi I had waiting for them. They didn't have much time before their flight left, so they had to hustle. The Swansons couldn't leave until tomorrow morning early, so they got an Uber to a hotel. I expect they're hiding out in their rooms right now.

"After your friends got out, the driver went to one of the hotels and took on more passengers before going to the airport. He seemed to enjoy the game we played with the press."

"Clever."

Belle's cell rang and she looked at the number. She sat up. "Colton?"

"Hi, sweetheart. I wanted to let you know we got home."

"Were you recognized?"

He laughed. "Reporters were at the airport, but Brian bought me a hoodie with a Colorado Rockies cap. You couldn't distinguish me from several other guys dressed similarly. We split up and met at the gate just in time to board."

"You're home now?"

"Yes. Our hunters show up tomorrow."

"Wow. Short turnaround time. Are you sure you're ready to go back into the mountains?"

"I'm tired. I've been eating every two hours, which helps. Just being home makes me feel better."

Dad mouthed, "Tell him about the interview."

"Colton, Dad set up an interview time with one of the network affiliates next week. Adam, Liam, and I will do video interviews. Will you be able to join us?"

"Doubtful, sweetheart."

Belle shook her head at her dad.

"Put him on speaker, Belle."

"Dad wants to talk to you."

"Colton?"

"Mr. St. John."

"Call me Jackson. Listen, members of the press are determined to interview you. If you can't make the video call, they may show up at the ranch."

Colton's abrupt laugh was not filled with humor. "The ranch is fenced, gated, under video surveillance, and far from any major city. They will not get in without an invitation."

"Do you want them to keep hounding you or your family? Your ability to survive a crash and fourteen days in the wilderness is nothing short of miraculous. You're major news."

He sighed. "All right. I'll have one of my brothers cover for me with the hunters. Send me the information. Belle knows my e-mail address." The unwillingness in his voice made Belle smile.

Dad nodded. "Good. At some point, you all will need to talk to that independent movie producer too. I have his contact information, and he has mine. Seems like a down-to-earth kind of guy. He suggests you all write down your memories while they are still fresh."

"Maybe." Colton's noncommittal tone made Belle grin. *He might consider this in a year or two—or maybe never.*

Dad left, and Belle took Colton off speaker. "I already miss you."

"I miss you too. Sleeping alone tonight is going to feel strange. I got used to three other people sharing heat and breathing space."

"Did your parents say anything to you about finding me in your bed?"

He laughed. "No, I'm thirty-three. They figure I can run my own life, but Brian had a lot to say about you being there. He shared the news with my other brothers and their wives as soon as he walked in the door. Your folks?"

"Oh, yes. They had something to say." She paused, and her tone sobered. "They don't understand, Colton. You are my safe place. Your heartbeat and scent calm me and give me hope. None of the reporters will understand either. I can guess the spin they might put on our situation, or the subtle suggestions they'll make if they find out we love each other. I can already see the headlines: 'Danger and Romance in the Rocky Mountains.' This makes me hesitant to interview."

"Just stick to the facts, Belle. That's what I intend to do. Keep the emotion out of your story."

Dad asked a news reporter from a local station to interview the survivors on behalf of the press.

"She frequents one of our restaurants, Belle, and your mom and I have gotten to know her over the last year. She's delighted to do this for us. We'll interview at their station tomorrow. I talked with Adam and Liam, and they have the video link to connect and the correct time for their time zone. Let's hope all their internet connections are stable, especially Colton's."

Lorra Webster chatted with Belle before the interview, and Belle relaxed. She'd dressed in her favorite black pencil dress and added a red silk scarf and string of pearls.

Fifteen minutes before they filmed, Lorra brought the others online to check the sound and video feeds.

Belle smiled to see them. "Hi, guys."

Adam gave her two thumbs up. "Looking good, Belle."

Liam agreed. Colton nodded and smiled.

He'd shaved and gotten a haircut, and she couldn't stop looking at him.

The corner of his lip curled, and she grinned.

Lorra straightened her jacket collar. "Okay, everyone. We're going live in a moment. Just relax. You'll be fine. We are pre-recording this interview for a special hour-long segment. I'll let you know when this will air."

When the cameras started rolling, Lorra reminded viewers of the date and location of the crash and what searchers had done when they first got word. She showed a video clip of one of the investigators explaining the process.

She continued. "Weather delayed the rescue for several days, but a Civil Air Patrol observer saw the downed plane just before they and the Search and Rescue teams were ready to call off the search."

A picture of the crash site with their suitcase arrow sobered Belle. She knew what lay under the brush near the plane. She wondered if the bodies had been removed yet.

Pictures and names of those who lost their lives were projected on a screen. Lorra's voice took on a solemn tone. "The co-pilot and seven other passengers did not survive, and we, at Channel 7 News and our affiliates, wish to extend our deepest condolences to their families.

"Captain Sutherland, you were a Navy fighter pilot for many years before you flew commercially, were you not? Can you tell us what happened? Take us step-by-step through the process."

Adam described air traffic control's instructions to reroute around the storm. "But the storm moved quickly, and lightning and hail surrounded us."

He explained how the plane responded after the lightning strike. He spoke with ease and confidence.

"Do you think a lightning strike brought you down?"

"Unlikely, but the investigators will determine the cause within the next several months."

"If you had to predict what they might find, what would you say?"

"Based on the unresponsive rudder and how the plane acted, my guess would be we had a midair collision, and whatever hit us damaged our vertical stabilizer."

Lorra's eyes widened. "Would you have felt this?"

"Not necessarily. We'd been rocked by turbulence for a half hour."

"Will you describe what happened after the crash?"

He did, and Belle relived the experience through his eyes. She could feel the color draining from her face as she remembered her pain and grief upon gaining consciousness.

Belle looked at Colton. His intense gaze reminded her to breathe. She took a deep breath and imagined his scent—pine trees, cold, and mountains—and the steady beat of his heart. She pulled that quietness inside her, and the color returned. He gave her a tiny nod.

"Captain Sutherland, do you credit the survival of your group to your specialized training as a soldier?"

Belle stared at Adam. What would he say?

"Though my training was invaluable, the mountain expertise of Colton Morgan was the deciding factor in our survival. We worked as a team and did what needed to be done."

"Thank you, Captain Sutherland. Mr. Morgan, you are a cattle rancher and hunting outfitter in Montana. Please tell us how the skills you developed in your occupation contributed to the welfare of the group. Will you give us specific examples?"

Colton gave her only what she asked for and no more. He told about starting the fires, building the shelters, making the heating container, and dealing with the injured elk, but he did not expand on the details. Did Lorra interpret Colton's minimal responses as passive-aggressive behavior? She hoped not.

"In your opinion, Mr. Morgan, which of the survivors contributed the most to the group's ability to stay positive and to hold onto hope?"

Without hesitation, Colton said, "Liam."

Belle and Adam nodded at his answer, and Lorra straightened. "Mr. Swanson—Liam. May I ask your age?"

"I'm twenty-one."

"And you're a Christian praise and worship leader?"

"Yes."

She raised a brow. "Does Mr. Morgan's answer surprise you?"

Liam smiled. "No, I suppose not. When things got tough, I reminded them that God knew exactly where we were and had a purpose for us. Somehow, we always found a way out."

"Can you give us specific examples?"

He nodded. "Early in our experience, Belle asked me to pray that searchers would find us while we were still alive, that her injury wouldn't get infected, and that we would get food soon. Against all odds, hunters found us alive, Belle's injury did not get infected, and she got food the next day," he grinned, "though the food wasn't what she expected."

He gave more examples.

"The fourteen days we spent in the mountains were filled with difficulties, uncertainty, cold, thirst, and hunger, but I saw many examples of God's loving kindness and mercy."

Lorra asked him a few more questions, and Belle knew she was next. Butterflies swarmed in her stomach.

CHAPTER 11

LORRA Webster smiled. "Thank you, Mr. Swanson." She turned to Belle. "Miss St. John, we've heard the details of the crash and the actions taken to ensure your survival, but we haven't heard the personal, emotional side of all this. Can you tell us what you felt? What stood out in your mind?"

Dread filled Belle, but she schooled her expression and glanced at the guys. Adam and Liam watched her, curiosity clear on their faces, but Colton's eyes warned her to be careful.

"I don't think I have the words to describe what I felt during those fourteen days, or what I'm feeling now, Miss Webster. I'm still trying to process everything."

"Will you try?"

"All right. When I first gained consciousness I felt pain, fear, and grief. I saw the wreckage and the loss of life. Before we crashed, I remember talking to one of the passengers across the aisle from me for most of the flight—a passenger who didn't survive. She was my age. Her death shocked me into the realization that mine could be just as close.

"We who survived were bloody and bruised, so you can imagine the aches and pains."

"You live in Dallas, Miss St. John. Have you had any mountain experience that prepared you for the last couple of weeks?"

Belle grimaced. "None. I was totally dependent on the men. They are my heroes. They cared for me and my injury, and they didn't get impatient when I made mistakes. I felt useless because I didn't have the slightest idea what to do to help us survive."

Lorra nodded encouragement. "Go on."

"When we reached the second camp, a place hunters had used, we found a few desperately needed supplies like water containers, pots, a few canned items, and a tarp. Adam set a trap for mice, and I cooked what we caught."

"You ate mice?"

"Yes. We faced starvation, Miss Webster, so we ate anything we could."

She smiled. "How did you, a connoisseur of fine foods, handle the first bite of mouse?"

The men chuckled at Lorra's question and waited for Belle's answer.

She grimaced. "Not well. Revulsion battled with my stomach's demand for protein. Liam helped me through the deciding moment. Eating mice and squirrels got easier after that. When we didn't have these and had only acorns and chokecherries, I wished for them."

The reporter nodded. "Mr. Swanson mentioned the cold. How did you protect yourself from hypothermia? I'm assuming you weren't dressed for the mountains."

Belle shook her head. “I wasn’t. Fortunately, we found our own pieces of luggage, so I could add layers.”

“What did you do at night?”

Belle’s middle tightened. “We covered ourselves with whatever extra clothing we could find and huddled together. At the second site, we found an old rubber blow-up mattress the hunters had placed over their stash before burying everything under logs. We used this to cover ourselves at night. I hope, when these hunters return to their camp, they’ll find the thank you note we left for them.

“At the third site, we heated rocks and let them warm our shelter.”

She didn’t want to continue in the direction the interview seemed to be going, so she addressed the reporter’s initial question. “You asked what stood out the most for me, and I’d have to say Liam’s singing. He sang for me whenever I felt anxious. He sang when we shelled acorns or had to remain inside the shelter because of the snow and had nothing to do but tell stories or listen to the wind soughing through the pine, fir, and aspen branches. He sang because song fills him and must come out. I could listen to Liam for hours. He has an amazing voice, and the words of his songs always brought peace.”

Liam wore a sheepish grin, but he took her praise in stride. She knew he immediately offered this to God and kept nothing for himself.

Lorra smiled. “One last question, Miss St. John. What else, besides Mr. Swanson’s songs, kept you from total panic?”

Belle smiled. "That's an easy question to answer, Miss Webster. My teammates included a highly skilled soldier, a man who talks to God, and an incredibly knowledgeable mountain man. No need to panic, right?"

Belle watched the interview on prime time the next week. She thought Lorra Webster had done a good job and hoped the reporters would be satisfied with the information she and the men had given and would leave them alone.

They weren't satisfied. A deluge of requests for additional interviews poured into the stations and were forwarded to Dad. The writer and movie producer contacted him directly and asked to meet with Belle. Both said they would be willing to travel to Dallas if necessary.

Adam and Liam videoconferenced with her soon after the interview aired.

"How are you, girlfriend? How are you holding up?" Adam grinned. "Are you getting enough to eat these days?"

"I'm fine, Adam, and you can bet I am. How about you?"

"I'm back to the weight I was before the crash."

"Did the investigators find out why we went down?"

Adam sobered. "They found another downed plane with debris spread over one hundred miles in our same area. The initial findings indicate we had a midair collision."

"Oh, no. More casualties?"

"Two. A man and his wife."

Belle rubbed her forehead. "Liam? How are you?"

"Fine, Belle. I'm scheduled to lead worship at a large conference in Dallas soon. If you don't mind putting me up, I'll fly out with Adam when he comes."

"Of course, you will stay with us. You have no choice. Let me know when you arrive, and we'll pick you up at the airport. We'll take you to dinner and get you where you need to go."

Adam grinned. "Did Colton see the interview?"

Belle shrugged. "I don't know. He and his brothers were packing the hunters and their meat out of the mountains. I expect him to call tonight."

Liam grimaced. "My folks and I have been snowed under with requests for more interviews. My inbox got so full, I maxed out the space. I got a new e-mail, so I sent you, Adam, and Colton my new one. For VIPs only."

Adam nodded. "I've hired my sister, Becca, to be my PR person. She's handling all the e-mails and calls."

Belle chewed on her bottom lip. "Dad says the movie director is eager to get more information from us. He says he's willing to travel to meet with us individually and will work with our schedules. What do you want Dad to tell him? Are you interested?"

Liam shifted in his chair. "I'm game for whatever you three want."

Adam nodded. "If you all decide to do this, then I'll agree. My guess is the producer will keep pushing until we give him an answer."

"Why don't I tell Dad to have him come when you are both here? I'm certain Colton won't talk to him unless given strong motivation to do so, but he won't stand in the way."

Liam chuckled. "If they are going to recreate some of the scenes, I'll be interested to see who they get to play all of us, especially Colton."

Belle laughed just as her cell rang. "I've got to go. Colton is on the line."

Adam lifted a hand. "Tell him we said hello."

"I will. Talk to you soon." She closed the chat and answered the call.

"Hi, love. I just got off a video call with Liam and Adam. They say hello. They'll be here in three weeks."

"How are you, sweetheart?"

"I'm fine. You sound tired."

"I am. As soon as I finish talking to you, I'm going to eat, shower, and go to bed."

"Why don't you call tomorrow and we can talk when you're not so tired."

"No, I want to hear your voice. I think I'm going to get another phone—one that lets me see your face while we're talking."

"Good idea. Get the same kind of phone I have, and we can FaceTime."

"Okay. Send me the info."

"Our interview aired. Did you get to see this?"

He sighed. "No, but that's all Brian has been talking about since I got in. You'd think he was a teenager instead of twenty-nine. He thinks we're going to be rich and famous. I think we're going to be bothered. Must be nice to have his enthusiasm. My folks recorded the show, so I'll watch when I'm not so tired."

"I hate to tell you this, but the interview created an avalanche of requests for more interviews."

"Oh, great." His unenthusiastic response made her smile.

"I miss you, Colton."

"I miss you, Belle. Every day we're apart, the stronger my need to hold you grows."

They chatted for several more minutes.

Belle stood. "I'm going to go now, love, so you can get some rest. Call me tomorrow so we can discuss a decision you, Liam, Adam, and I need to make."

"All right, sweetheart. I love you."

Colton called early the next morning, just as Belle got out of the shower. She wrapped a towel around herself and answered. "Hey, love. Did you get enough rest?"

"Yes. I have a week off before the next three hunters show up. A couple of the horses need to be shod before we take them into the mountains, so my older brothers and I will put their shoes on this afternoon. What's up with the others?"

Belle related the conversation.

Colton sighed. "I don't suppose they're going to give up any time soon, so if you want to talk to the producer, I'm fine with this."

"He'll want to talk to you too."

"Not on my schedule, unless he pays the fee and I haul him to the mountains."

She laughed. "As eager as he is, he just might agree. Did you watch the interview yet?"

"Yes, while I ate breakfast."

"What did you think? How did I do?"

"You did well, sweetheart. I couldn't take my eyes off you the whole time."

"Same here. I like the haircut, by the way. You looked like a movie star."

"Oh, please, Belle. You're yanking my chain, aren't you?"

She laughed. "Just a little."

Belle and Adam sat across the table from producer Randy Willis in a back room in one of Dad's restaurants. Liam and her father sat on each side of him.

Willis was a well-dressed man in his late forties. Gray streaked the hair at his temples, though the rest of his hair was thick and black. "Thank you for that delicious meal. I also want to thank you all for agreeing to meet with me. Your story has the potential to inspire millions around the globe."

Adam placed his napkin on the table. "Why us, Mr. Willis? Others have survived plane crashes, but documentaries haven't always been made about them."

"That is a fair question, Captain Sutherland. My co-producers and I thought your story had unique qualities, especially after we got reports of how many viewers watched your interview. Social media posts about your rescue are going viral. One site has more than a million views. We can't ignore this information."

Adam took the lead in the conversation. "So, tell us what you want from us."

Willis leaned forward his eyes full of eagerness. "We want to tell your stories. To do this accurately, I need detailed information only you can provide. I'd like to set up a series of interviews over the next several months if you contract with me."

He opened his briefcase and pulled out legal documents. "I'm sure you'll want your attorneys to look these over before signing. My business card with my contact number is attached. I'll send Mr. Morgan his in the next mail. He's a hard man to connect with. I hope he'll agree to talk to me."

Belle smiled. "Do you know how to ride horses, Mr. Willis?"

"I've been on one a time or two."

"Well, you might consider calling the ranch and scheduling a trip to the mountains. My guess is that's the only way you're going to have Colton's undivided attention."

Belle answered Colton's FaceTime call. "Hey, you. How did the pack with Mr. Willis go?"

"Better than I expected. He brought his co-producer and a camera guy. Though they weren't hunting, I packed them as if they were. We camped for a couple of days. They were saddle sore and limped after a two-day ride from and to the ranch, but they didn't complain. For city guys, they weren't bad. They shot a lot of video.

"I showed them how to make a fire and build shelters like we used. My conscience wouldn't let me make them go hungry after they gave me such a large tip, so they ate better than we did in Colorado, though I did prepare mice for one of the meals."

She laughed. "Did he ask you a lot of questions?"

"Yes. More than I wanted to answer. He said Adam gave him the coordinates to each of our camps, and as soon as he left me, he, the director, and a couple of videographers planned to go to Colorado to trace our steps and to get footage, assuming the weather doesn't shut them down."

"Is he on to us?"

"No, not unless he talked to Brian. I enlisted my other brothers' help to keep our youngest occupied. One of the hunters who showed up is an attractive woman, and Brian was given the job of guiding her. He's thrilled."

"Smart move."

"I think so. Are you back to work?"

Belle nodded. "On a part-time basis. I can't walk down the street openly anymore because someone recognizes me and approaches. Paparazzi are always around. I don't know why this bothers me so much. I've been in the spotlight before, but Dallas doesn't feel like home now."

He smiled. "I have a solution for that, sweetheart. Move to Montana. The air is clean and fresh, and the people are great—one man, in particular, has a place for you."

She smiled. "I'm seriously considering such a move. I'm researching the state now."

He chuckled. "What kind of research?"

"Oh, the basics—crime rate, climate, population, nearest airports, cost of living, property values, water quality, closest restaurants, current businesses, and the possible need for new businesses. Dad might be interested in opening a restaurant. I even got a book on edible plants in the Montana high country."

"Why did you do that?"

She hesitated. "I've been having dreams about our time in the mountains. I'm cold and hungry and looking for something to eat. When I eat plants, they're always poisonous, and I'm about to die. I figured if I learned about edible plants, I'd stop having the bad dreams."

"When you get here, talk to my sister-in-law, Grace. She's a forager."

"I'd love to talk to her."

Colton studied her face. "I miss you, Belle. I'm counting down the weeks until you get here."

"I miss you too, love. Thanksgiving is a couple of weeks away. What are you and your family doing?"

"We don't have hunters during Thanksgiving week, so we take care of stock and equipment and relax a little.

"Mom and my sisters-in-law cook and clean and get the house ready for a large crowd. I'm sure you can imagine the aroma.

"Two weeks later, they and the kids decorate the place for Christmas."

Belle smiled. "Now that you have your new phone, will you take videos and pictures and send them to me?"

"Sure."

"Mom. Dad. I've made up my mind. When Colton asks me to marry him again, I'm going to say yes."

Dad studied her face. "Are you sure this is what you want, hon? Your life will be drastically different."

"Yes, this is what I want. Though I love you and our home here, Dallas isn't as welcoming anymore. Being in the mountains changed me. I can't describe this change, but I feel the effects every day."

Tears fell from Mom's eyes. "Montana is so far away, darling. We'll miss you."

Belle chuckled. "Don't cry, Mom. A direct flight from Dallas to Glacier Park International Airport will take you about four hours in the corporate jet."

CHAPTER 12

BELLE studied the landscape as they taxied to a stop. Her heart raced and her lungs demanded air. Several inches of snow covered the ground, but the sun shone on the surface and created diamond crystals.

Colton said he'd be waiting for them outside the front doors of the terminal.

He greeted her parents, then took her into his arms and whispered, "You are more beautiful each time I see you, Belle. For the past week, my gut wouldn't settle knowing you were coming. When we get out of public view, I have three months of stored kisses to give you." He lowered his head and kissed her. "That's the first one."

Belle put her arms around his neck and returned his kiss.

He loaded the suitcases and slid into the driver's seat of a silver SUV. The name of their outfitting business on the front doors identified them, and Belle wondered if local reporters were on the lookout for Colton.

Mom smiled. "Nice to see you again. I hope having us here isn't inconvenient."

"No, Mrs. St. John, we have plenty of room, and my family is looking forward to showing you a great time."

"Call me Holly."

He nodded. "Holly."

Belle scanned the people around them. "Do the reporters leave you alone?"

"Mostly. My parents or brothers typically come into town for any errands, so they don't expect me. I'm hoping their interest will die down soon."

Dad chuckled. "Unlikely. The more interviews Randy Willis and his people do with Belle, Liam, and Adam, the more interest and questions they have. Your elusiveness excites their interest. They got funding for the documentary and are not wasting any time starting the process."

"Did they retrace our steps?"

"Yes, they hired a local outfitter to take them in. Willis is delighted with the footage they have so far. He's interviewed the hunters who brought you out and the hospital staff who cared for you."

"What about that author? The ghostwriter?"

Mom chuckled. "She's enthusiastic to say the least. She convinced Belle to meet with her."

"And?"

Belle shrugged. "Her name is Amber Morris. Amber is soft-spoken and likeable. She seems to be fascinated with my side of our story."

Colton turned to her. "How well does she write? Do you know?"

"Yes. I've read two other books she's ghostwritten. They're excellent. I told her I'd get back to her after

Christmas with my decision. I think this could be a fun project."

Mom studied all the lighting and decorations as they drove through town. "Looks like people go all out here for Christmas."

Colton smiled. "They do. Tomorrow afternoon, they'll have a parade downtown. In the evening, they'll light the huge tree. If you're interested in shopping, the business district and restaurants will stay open late."

Mom eyed an antique shop as they passed. "Sounds fun. I'd like to. Can you recommend any of the restaurants?"

"We have several popular hangouts—burgers, Chinese, Mexican, and pizza places—but nothing you're probably used to."

Dad studied the businesses. "Might be nice for a change—unless your parents have something else planned?"

"They hoped the town celebration would interest you. They wanted you to experience the fun."

They drove for forty-five minutes before Colton turned through an impressive log entry. At a push of a button, the heavy metal gates closed behind them.

Belle gazed at everything around her. This would be her new home. The quietness of the snow-covered place called to the quietness her mountain experience left inside her. She relaxed.

She eyed the large log building with interest. The place looked like a Christmas postcard or a Thomas Kincaid painting.

Mom gasped. "Charming."

He pulled into a large log garage and shut off the engine. His eyes met hers. "We're home."

Belle looked into his face and whispered, "Home. My new favorite word."

His green gaze intensified and filled with a question.

Belle smiled and nodded, and his eyes widened.

He got out of the vehicle and hurried around to open her door, while his brothers and parents greeted her parents and helped them with their luggage.

Janet pointed. "Holly, you and Jackson come inside and warm up. We have appetizers ready."

Her parents followed the Morgans inside.

Colton touched her face. "Does the soft way you said home mean what I think this means?"

"Yes, love."

His arms went around her, and he rested his forehead against hers. "You'll marry me, Belle?"

"Yes."

He shared hungry kisses number two, three, and four with her.

Belle put a hand to his cheek. "We'd better get inside. They'll wonder what's happened to us."

He chuckled. "I'm sure they know what's happened to us, but I should take you inside so the rest of my family can meet you."

The interior of the home felt just as she imagined once she saw the pictures Colton sent—warm and friendly. She smiled at the aroma of roasting meat, vegetables, pine boughs, and cinnamon-scented candles, and gazed at the lights and huge Christmas tree *Home. Love. Family.* The thoughts settled into her soul.

"Belle, this is my older brother, Bill, and his wife, Laura. Standing beside them are my next older brother, Charlie, and his wife, Grace. You already know Brian.

Brian grinned and hugged her. "Welcome to our home, Belle. We've been looking forward to seeing you."

"Thank you."

He stepped back, and she gazed at the men and women who would be her brothers- and sisters-in-law. "I'm pleased to meet you all."

Colton tilted his head. "And the two teen boys over at the table trying to sneak food are Landon and Joseph.

"Boys, come over here and meet our guests. Bring your cousins with you." He pointed. "Kirk and Danny are the ten-year-old twins, and the two girls are Wren and Christy. Landon and the twins belong to Bill and Laura, and the others belong to Charlie and Grace."

She smiled.

The older boys walked over with the younger children.

Belle offered her hand and shook each of theirs. "I'm happy to meet you all."

The young ones greeted her, then ran off to play.

Landon eyed her, appreciation in his eyes. "Uncle Brian said you looked like a supermodel. He wasn't lying."

Joseph grinned. "He wasn't, was he?"

Colton took Belle's hand. "Come, I'll show you to your room."

Janet tilted her head at him. "Don't dawdle, Son. We're going to have an early dinner."

"Okay, Mom."

Belle followed him up the carpeted stairs and into a warm and friendly room. Pine garlands wrapped with tiny lights and crimson and gold ribbons draped the wardrobe and windows.

He set her suitcases on the floor and put his arms around her. "I hoped you would say yes to me, Belle, so I got a special license and talked to a local minister. He said he could marry us the morning following Christmas Day.

"Bill said he would be our photographer. He's better than good. Many of his wildlife photographs show up in magazines all over the country. He's also a talented videographer. Would you consider this, sweetheart, or do you need more time?"

She brushed back a lock of his hair. "I told Mom and Dad I would say yes to you when you asked. We discussed the possibility you might want to get married during the holiday, so I planned for this.

"Dad asked me to get you to come to Dallas for a reception after the first of the year. He said this is the least we could do. Mom is already happily planning the party."

Colton grimaced. "All right. I'll be way out of my comfort zone, so I'll depend on my wife to help me navigate such a large, dangerous city, as well as all the social protocols."

"I will, my elusive mountain man."

The whole town turned out for the parade and tree lighting. Mom and Dad oohed and ahhed over the quaintness and beauty of everything they saw. Their relaxed postures made Belle smile.

After a tasty dinner at the town's only upscale grill, they strolled the sidewalks and visited several stores. Carolers sang to passers-by, and vendors sold hot chocolate and apple cider.

"Mom, Belle and I will wait for you by the Christmas tree." Colton intertwined his fingers with hers.

"Okay. We'll be there in about fifteen."

Belle looked into the clear night sky and inhaled. "This place is so beautiful."

He led her to the back of the Christmas tree, away from the crowds, and reached inside the pocket of his sheepskin coat. He pulled out a red jewelry box. "I want to make this official, Belle." He knelt on one knee and opened the box. "Will you marry me?"

She touched his face. "Yes, love."

He slid the diamond ring on her finger, then stood and gave her more of the saved kisses.

Bill walked up, camera in hand. "I got some excellent shots of the proposal. I want to get more of you kissing when they light the tree, and I want up-close shots of the engagement ring too."

Belle's heart raced. She had just turned the page of her life to a new chapter. She smiled. Life was good.

Someone knocked on her bedroom door. Belle opened one eye and glanced at the clock. 7:00 a.m. The sun hadn't lit the sky yet.

She sat up. "Who's there?"

"Colton."

"Come in."

He strode in dressed in a red plaid shirt, jeans, and boots. Her fiancé looked like he'd been up for a couple of hours.

"What's wrong, love?"

He sat on the edge of her bed and stroked her cheek. "I have good news and bad. Which do you want to hear first?"

"The good news."

"Breakfast is ready."

"The bad?"

"Someone took photos when we kissed at the airport. This same person and a few of her friends must have followed us around town yesterday. They got pictures as we strolled hand-in-hand, kissed, and I asked you to marry me. The images are all over the internet."

He sighed. "Adam texted and said thousands have seen the pictures already and made comments. They're resharing the images with everybody. At this rate, he thinks the posts will go viral by the end of today. People are asking a lot of questions and wondering what really happened in the mountains. What do they want us to say? That we had some kind of illicit affair?

"Your dad said the first text he got this morning was from Randy Willis wanting to know if he could schedule more interviews. He thinks the pictures add human interest to the story they want to tell.

"That television news reporter, Lorra Webster, also texted and asked for another interview. She said calls and e-mails are pouring in from all over the country."

He groaned. “This makes me tired, Belle. Why won’t people leave us alone?”

She knew how much her mountain man valued his privacy and how much he hated being the subject of gossip. “Leaving us alone isn’t in their nature, love. They think they have a right to know everything about everything.”

He cupped her cheek. “Maybe we can take a couple of horses and slip into the mountains for a few hours. I need to clear my head. I’ve got a horse I think you’ll like.”

Belle threw back the covers and stood. “As long as we have plenty of food, something hot to drink, and warm clothes, I’m game. Give me a few minutes to change. I’ll meet you downstairs.”

“I’ll saddle the horses and pack a lunch.”

Bill asked to ride with them so he could get several winter pictures, and she and Colton agreed.

He grinned. “You’re both quite photogenic, you know? You make my life as a photographer easier.”

Colton snorted, but Belle smiled. “Thank you for doing this for us, Bill.”

Belle admired the men’s easy postures and natural grace as they rode. She marveled at how well they fit in this rugged environment and wondered if she would ever be at ease in such a setting.

The creak of leather, the occasional jingle of spurs, and the sight of the horses’ breaths in the cold air as they moved through the snow imprinted on her mind. This was true beauty.

After Bill got the shots he wanted, he returned to the ranch.

They rode another thirty minutes before Colton stopped and dismounted. He came around to her and helped her down. "I'll build a fire. We'll give the horses a breather."

He removed a magnesium striker and a handful of what looked like a small bird's nest from his saddlebag. In moments, he'd kindled a fire in a previously used fire pit and opened a thermos of coffee. He poured her a cup, and they both sat on logs.

"What should we do about the uninvited attention we're getting, Belle? I'm out of my element here."

She shrugged. "Nothing we can do but ignore everything and focus on us. I asked Dad, Liam, and Adam to tell those requesting interviews we won't be available until the middle of January."

"Do you want to go anywhere for our honeymoon?"

She watched his face. "No. Maybe we can visit Glacier and Yellowstone Parks in the summer. What do you think?"

His relieved smile made her grin. "Perfect."

"One of these days, I'll take you to Switzerland to see the Alps. You'll appreciate them."

He grinned and handed her a scrambled egg sandwich. "As long as I can get there without flying. I can't say I'm eager to get on a plane anytime soon."

Belle took a bite. "Yum. This is much better than fried mice any day."

He laughed and bit into his sandwich. “Agreed, though the mice weren’t that bad. Hunger changes a person’s mindset.”

She studied his face as she ate.

Colton raised his brows. “What? Why are you looking at me like that? I am not an expert in the art of reading your expressions yet, so tell me.”

Belle tilted her head. “I remember what I first thought about you—all the faulty assumptions I made—and how wrong I was. I love you, Colton Morgan.”

He stood and offered her a hand.

She put hers in his, and he helped her stand.

His arms went around her. “I love you too, Belle. I’m the luckiest man alive to have someone as special as you agree to marry me.” He placed her hand inside his coat and over his heart. “Do you feel the pounding?”

She nodded and rested against him.

Fat, lazy snowflakes fell around them.

Colton stepped back and looked at the sky. “We’d better head back. Are you ready?”

“I’m ready.”

They mounted and cantered home.

Belle gazed at herself in the long mirror and tried to calm the tremors in her stomach. Today, she would become Mrs. Arabella Morgan.

Mom stepped up beside her and adjusted Belle’s white faux fur collar. “You are absolutely stunning, darling. You epitomize the Christmas bride. Your form-fitting cocktail dress and white cropped fur jacket were the right choices."

Belle glanced at her image one more time. The upswept hair style and diamond jewelry emphasized the glow in her cheeks and the excitement in her eyes.

Mom handed her the bouquet of red roses and baby's breath. "Ready?"

"Yes. Let's go."

Dad waited for her. His eyes teared when he offered her his arm. "My beautiful girl."

Landon and Charlie seated the Morgans and Mom, then stood at the front of the church with Colton, while Bill snapped photos from different angles. Her two sisters-in law stood as her matrons of honor. Belle anticipated getting to know them better.

The bridal march started, and Belle stepped forward with Dad.

Colton's eyes shone, and he smiled as she walked toward him.

Belle thought he looked fabulous in a tailored suit and tie, but she pushed down the thought that she much preferred the untamed cowboy mountain man look.

Dad placed her hand in Colton's and the ceremony began.

The minister smiled. "I now pronounce you husband and wife. Colton, you may kiss your bride."

Colton didn't hesitate. He kissed her with enthusiasm and passion, and the family members cheered.

He whispered near her ear. "Do you think Bill has enough pictures yet?" He tugged at his collar. "I want to get out of this suit."

She laughed. "No, we still have to cut the cake back at the ranch."

They turned and walked down the aisle.

He grinned. "When they have their mouths full, let's slip away upstairs."

"Let's do."

Belle sipped hot chocolate and gazed at the computer screen.

The door opened, and Colton stepped in from outside. He brought the scent of pine trees, cold, and horses with him. He kissed her. "You're up early, wife. What are you reading?"

She poured him a cup of coffee. "I sent Lorra Webster a few of Bill's beautiful wedding photos to post on their news site. Look."

He stood behind her shoulder and read aloud.

Beauty and the Mountain Man

> December 26
>
> Mr. and Mrs. Jackson St. John and Mr. and Mrs. Henry Morgan are pleased to announce the marriage of their children, Arabella St. John and Colton Morgan.
>
> The couple met high in the Colorado Rockies after their plane crashed. For the next fourteen days, they and two others struggled to survive.

The article summarized their experience and finished with wishes for their happiness in Montana and a request for another interview.

Belle pointed. “Look. Almost half a million people have liked and shared the post, and they put the pictures up only yesterday.”

He frowned as he read some of the comments. “They want to know more. They’re speculating about our relationship in the mountains and asking for the ‘untold’ story. They want the station to do follow-up interviews.” He brushed a hand through his hair. “We’ll never be done with this, will we?”

“They’ll eventually focus on something else, but I think the answer is to let Amber Morris write our story. Then we can interview as soon as the book releases, and we’ll tell interested people where to get their copy if they want more details. What do you think? She sent me a message this morning. She’s ready to start.”

He smiled. “I like that idea. Have you thought of a title?”

She turned and put her arms around his waist. “How about *Belle and the Mountain Man: An Unlikely Romance*?”

He grinned. “Sounds like a book I just might read.”

ABOUT THE AUTHOR

DERINDA BABCOCK is an author and graphic designer. She lives in southwestern Colorado near the base of the western slope of the Rocky Mountains. In her previous career as an English as a Second Language teacher, she worked with students of all ages and many different linguistic and cultural backgrounds. The richness of this experience lends flavor and voice to the stories she writes. You can contact her at www.derindababcock.com/contact/

THE
JINDENTORS
A TALE OF THREE KINGDOMS
BOOK 1
DERINDA BABCOCK

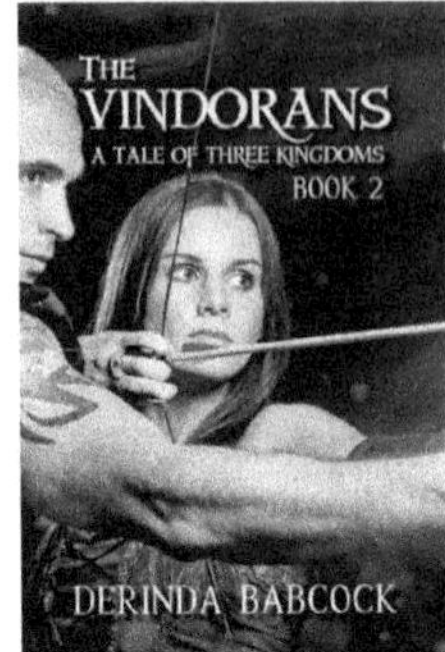
THE
VINDORANS
A TALE OF THREE KINGDOMS
BOOK 2
DERINDA BABCOCK

THE
BINROMESE
A TALE OF THREE KINGDOMS
BOOK 3
DERINDA BABCOCK

DODGING
DESTINY
DERINDA BABCOCK

IN SEARCH OF
DESTINY
DESTINY TRILOGY BOOK 2
SECOND EDITION

DESTINY TRILOGY BOOK 3
FOLLOWING
DESTINY
DERINDA BABCOCK

HUNTING FOR
DESTINY
A DESTINY TRILOGY
NOVELLA
DERINDA BABCOCK

VOICES FROM THE
PAST
A DESTINY TRILOGY
CHRISTMAS SHORT STORY
DERINDA BABCOCK

TREASURES OF THE HEART BOOK 1
COLORADO
TREASURE
SECOND EDITION
DERINDA BABCOCK

TREASURES OF THE HEART BOOK 2
TROUBLE in
TEXAS
COMING
DERINDA BABCOCK

TREASURES OF THE HEART BOOK 3
The PRODIGAL
RETURNS
COMING
DERINDA BABCOCK

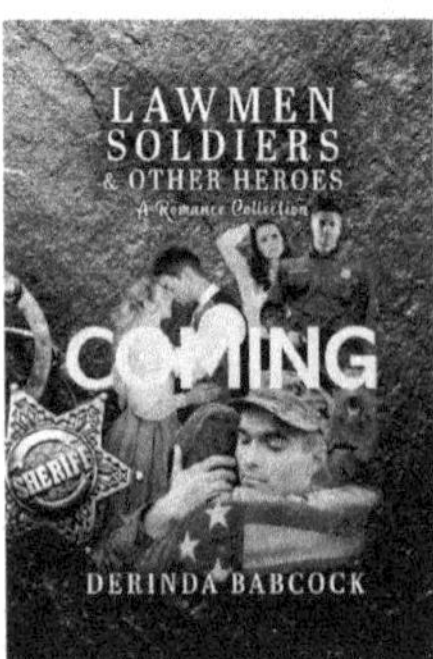
LAWMEN
SOLDIERS
& OTHER HEROES
A Romance Collection
COMING
SHERIFF
DERINDA BABCOCK

DERINDA'S OTHER BOOKS

A Tale of Three Kingdoms Series

The Jindentors (audiobook available), Book 1

The Vindorans, (audiobook available) Book 2

The Binromese (audiobook in process), Book 3

The Destiny Series

Dodging Destiny (audiobook available), Book 1

In Search of Destiny, Book 2

Following Destiny, Book 3

Hunting for Destiny (novella), Book 4

Voices from the Past (short story), Book 5

Treasures of the Heart trilogy:

Colorado Treasure (audiobook available), Book 1

Trouble in Texas (coming soon), Book 2

The Prodigal Returns (coming soon), Book 3

Lawmen, Soldiers, & Other Heroes: A Romance Collection (coming soon)

NOTE TO READER

If you enjoyed *Things Not Seen*, please post an online review on Amazon and/or Goodreads. Thanks! Your opinion matters.

www.ingramcontent.com/pod-product-compliance
Lightning Source LLC
Chambersburg PA
CBHW070628310726
48982CB00001B/201
* 9 7 8 0 9 9 0 4 3 9 8 8 2 *